Rebel in Petticoats

NANCY GENTRY

Rebel in Petticoats

NANCY GENTRY

To Anne,
You are such an inspiration
to me!
Nancy Gentry

O'MORE
PUBLISHING

FRANKLIN, TENNESSEE

Rebel in Petticoats

Copyright © 2008 by Nancy Gentry
ISBN-10   0-9800285-6-6
ISBN-13   978-0-9800285-6-0

Edited by Jessa Rose Sexton
Cover design by Amy Davidson
Book Block design by Joanna Arnold, Amy Davidson,
Ashlea Nippers, and Amanda Smith
Art Direction by Paula Rozelle Hanback
Illustrations by Jayne Williams

Published by:
O'More Publishing
A Division of O'More College of Design
423 South Margin St.
Franklin, TN 37064 U.S.A.

In memory of my dad, Jim Henry Burks

Contents

Acknowledgements

Many, many thanks go to Jessa Sexton who liked my story and put much time and effort into getting it ready for press. Being a creative writer herself and having a meticulous eye for detail, she brought a high level of expertise to this project. Working with her has been an absolute joy.

I would also like to thank Paula Hanback and her students Amy Davidson, Joanna Arnold, Ashlea Nippers, and Amanda Smith from O'More College of Design for all the talent and energy they put into designing the book and cover. Together they did an outstanding job of which I am very proud. I couldn't have asked for a better team.

My husband, Earl, gets all the credit for changing my dream of this book into reality. I thank him for not letting me hide my story on a shelf to collect dust. His continued encouragement helped me to step into new territory, and his support has been, and always will be, all-important to me.

Because my family plays such a major role in my life, I thank my mother, sister, daughters, and granddaughters for their guidance, inspiration, and enthusiasm. Sharing my experiences with them makes everything fun and more meaningful. Thanks also to good friends who have encouraged and supported me.

In 1860 ten-year-old Rachel Franklin lived in a world so different from ours today that it would seem to be a different planet. The earth was a quieter place. The peacefulness was never broken by the sounds of cell phones, televisions, car engines, or overhead airplanes. Grass and dirt had not yet disappeared under blankets of pavement. Life moved slowly. News and people traveled only as quickly as the speediest horse or steam locomotive. It was a peaceful, happy life on the Franklin's southern plantation. Like the other elite families who lived in the south, they enjoyed a legacy of wealth, power, and privilege that had been passed down through generations. Their culture, unique to the southern states of this earlier America, had existed for almost 200 years. They were a proud people who believed their way of life was right and just and moral, and it was their duty to preserve it.

In truth, however, there were areas of southern living that were neither right nor just nor moral. The scale of equality was so totally unbalanced that only about 40,000 plantation owners controlled nearly 4 million enslaved people. These people were descendants of Africans brought to America nearly 200 years earlier. Generations of them had labored on the plantations making the South prosperous. They were a strong people who endured daily hardships and survived. They were an intelligent people, managing to piece together the English language with no education or help, resulting in a dialect unique to their race. They were a resourceful people, creating a life for themselves as best they could within the confines of slavery.

By 1860 masters and slaves had co-existed since birth, as their parents and grandparents had done. It was the only life either side had ever known. For the powerful southern planters an end to slavery meant the collapse of southern life. To understand this idea is to understand the friction between North and South. For decades northern people had pushed to do away with slavery, but the southern people had been too powerful. With expansion of the United States into the territories west of the Mississippi River, the issue of slavery became of vital importance. Would the new states be slave or free? This one question sparked intense passion and fury on both sides, often ending in fighting and bloodshed. Many southern people no longer saw Northerners as their fellow Americans. An enormous gap had grown between the two cultures, and Southerners believed their whole existence was

being threatened. They felt they could no longer live in harmony with the North.

The election of Abraham Lincoln as President in 1860 caused the final snap of their already strained, tense relations. They could not understand why the President would not let them withdraw from the Union peacefully, but they were willing to fight what they believed would be a brief battle to protect their way of life. The southern states began to pull out of the Union in rapid order. They hated Lincoln and refused to remain under a government that might take away their way of life, values, homes, prosperity, and freedom to make any decisions that may differ from Northerners' viewpoint.

As the war began and progressed, hatred on both sides deepened toward one another. The vile Yankees were an enemy who dared to invade the Southerners' homeland. On the other side, people from the North believed the evil 'secesh' deserved to have their homeland destroyed. It was the darkest time in America's history.

Because it is our American history, it deserves our study. We can learn from our ancestors and turn the course of our own lives. We can look at the great leaders, like Abraham Lincoln, and the heroes who emerged from this time and model ourselves after them. We can marvel at how our people were able to right a terrible wrong and how far we have come since then. We can admire the generation of people who were caught up in the changing of an era, suffered through it, and survived.

1
A Mad Dog Night

april, 1863

IT WAS AN EERIE NIGHT. The moon was perfectly round and bright white, so bright that it cast shadows of the trees on the dusty dirt road ahead. Rachel could see the two mules in front of her, their floppy ears and bristly manes, their bulky harnesses and rein straps, as clearly as if it were dusk instead of well past midnight.

The road was badly rutted, and the wagon pitched and jolted its two passengers. Josup gripped the reins tightly, jiggling them nervously and clucking quietly to keep the mules at a steady pace.

"Dis a night da mad dogs run," he whispered.

Rachel stole a quick glance at Josup then focused her eyes back on the road. His eyes were big, and the whites of them were as bright white as the moon. He had beads of sweat on his wrinkled brow, although the wind was breezy and cool. His chin was whiskered with tiny white stubble that matched the white curly stubble on his head. His dark skin was leathery but thin, and it was stretched over jaws that were clenched tightly together. Poor old Josup was as frightened as she was.

Rachel gripped the metal sidearm tightly as a wheel dropped in another deep rut, bumping her up off the seat. Her eyes darted from side to side, and her ears strained to hear any sound beyond the creaky wagon and trodding mules. She thought about what Josup had just said. It wasn't mad dogs she was worried about. She remembered seeing one once, growling, frothing white at the mouth, eyes filled with hatred, a terrible sight. But she would gladly face a dozen mad dogs tonight rather than what could be in store for her.

Rachel thought of her home and her parents. Her mind was still reeling from all the events that had taken place this night. Or was it the same night? Could so much have happened in only one night? It seemed impossible, but she knew that it was true. She tried to go over everything again in her mind. It had all happened so quickly. The look on her mother's beautiful face, stone cold and unafraid as she faced the Yankee's gun, burned in Rachel's mind. Her stomach still ached from the sight of her father's blood. And the unbelievable fright that filled her body when the Yankee soldiers burst into her house was still sending cold chills up and down her spine.

Just then, one of the mules stumbled. Its sleepy partner was startled and brayed loudly, cutting the silence of the night like a knife. Metal clanged. Hooves clamored in a cloud of dust, ready to bolt. Josup's body jerked as he struggled to gain control of the spooked animals. His deep voice and strong hands soon calmed the mules, and they all sat still for a few minutes to catch their breaths.

Rachel spun around on the wood-plank seat and stared into the darkness behind them. If soldiers were there, they would surely have heard the commotion. Her ears strained to hear any hint of horses' hooves. All she could hear was the beating of her own heart as it pounded in her ears.

"Easy, missy," comforted Josup.

At first, Rachel thought he was still talking to the mules. "Ain't nothin' comin'."

Then she knew he was speaking to her, trying to soothe her nerves as well as his own, she supposed.

Rachel tried to answer, but her voice was tied in a knot in her throat, and nothing would come out. In silence she sat looking straight ahead. She fought the urge to look back at the road again or in the trees beside the road that rustled with the breeze as they passed. Focusing her eyes on the big ears of the mules, she wished they could fly — or at least go faster. She had to make it in time. It was a matter of life or death, the lives of so many good men, sons, fathers, brothers. And her own life as well.

Rachel thought of the piece of paper sewn to her petticoat. It felt as if it were burning a hole right through

3

her skirt. She tried hard not to think about it because she knew what it meant for her if the Yankees were to find out. Not only would she be unable to warn her father's men and deliver his plan to them, she would be declared a Confederate spy and hanged from the nearest tree. The Yankees were ruthless and vile, and they wouldn't care that she was only twelve years old.

Rachel looked at Josup's dark, leathery hands as they held the reins. They were trembling, and she knew it was not from the strain but from fear. He had no reason to fear for his own life because they both knew the Yankees would set Josup free. But he was afraid for her. He was afraid for her mother and father, the only family he had ever known, and what might happen to all of them. For an instant Rachel was filled with a warmth of love for Josup, and she was comforted. She wanted to pat his hand and say that everything would be fine. But she could not utter words that she didn't believe, not to Josup, not to herself.

The warm feeling left Rachel as quickly as it had come, and she felt fear creep through her body again, making her spine tingle and the fine hairs on her arm stand on end. She shuddered and clutched her arms. She might be only twelve, but she was on a grown-up's mission, and she knew she would be treated as one by the enemy.

Rachel squeezed her eyes shut and rubbed her forehead that was beginning to throb from the strain. She tried to imagine that she was on a pleasant buggy ride with her father, the kind of ride they used to take in that world before the war.

4

Life had not always been so dreadful and frightening and miserable. She remembered a time, only two years ago but seeming like a hundred, when men took guns to hunt deer instead of other men, when women shed tears over silly love stories or broken vases instead of the loss of a husband or son. Grief was everywhere, and no one, not the rich nor the well-bred, was spared. It was now a way of life. And Rachel tried never to allow herself to think back on the good life that was wiped out with this wretched war. There was no going back. Things would never be so simple and happy again. And it was too painful to think about it.

But tonight, as she tried to block out all the events that had happened and might yet happen, as she tried not to feel the heavy burden of her task and the terrible consequences if she failed, she allowed her memories to emerge. Rachel closed her eyes again and seemed to float off the hard, wood seat as she remembered a warm spring day. She could almost feel the fresh breeze on her cheek and smell the scent of honeysuckle mixed with the familiar smells of horses, dirt, and freshly baked bread. She could almost hear the soft rustle of her mother's big skirt as she moved busily inside the house. On that day, a long time ago, life was free of worries for a little girl, and the world was beautiful.

2
The Fight's On, Boys!

april 14, 1861

"FOR DA LAWD… SAID… UN… TO MOSES," the young girl took a deep breath and brushed a fly off the page from which she was reading. There were tiny sweat beads on her forehead although it was a pleasant spring day, and the breeze was cool on the back porch. She was doing some powerful hard thinking.

"Keep goin'," whispered Rachel. Her head of soft brown curls was pressed against her friend's head which was wrapped tightly in a kerchief. Both pairs of eyes were focused on the old Bible that lay across their laps.

Lizbet cleared her throat. "Go on… un… to… puh… puh … "

"Not 'puh'," Rachel corrected her. "It's p-h, and it sounds like *f-f-f.*"

Rachel put her upper teeth on her bottom lip and puffed. "*F-f-f-f,* like in fish."

Lizbet scrunched her nose and scratched her head. She imitated Rachel's mouth and made the sound. Then she looked hard at the word on the page and shook her head in frustration.

"I stuck," Lizbet sighed and took another deep breath. "I can't get dis one."

Rachel put her finger under the word and said, "Pharaoh."

Lizbet's eyes widened, and her eyebrows shot up. The look on her face was so surprised and funny that Rachel giggled. But before Lizbet could get started again on her reading lesson a voice from inside the house called.

"Ra-a-chel, come to dinner. Rachel, where are you? Come to dinner."

It was Rachel's mother, and this was the second time she had called.

"Yes, ma'am, I'm comin'," Rachel said in a very soft and weak voice. Then she nudged Lizbet and said, "Go on. Keep readin'."

Rachel loved her time with Lizbet. She was the only friend Rachel had for miles around. Lizbet was a slave child, the same age as Rachel. She had been born and raised on their plantation, as well as her mother, Lily, before her. But Lizbet had no school to attend. The only schooling she had came from Rachel's mother. And Rachel loved to help. She loved to share the old Bible sto-

ries she learned each Sunday at church and to help Lizbet read them.

The two girls were best friends. Different as night and day, but best friends nevertheless. It was not only the color of their skin that made them different, but everything about them. Lizbet was tall for her age and very thin. Her legs looked like two bean poles with long, flat feet at the bottom to hold them up. Her hair was always knotted into tiny braids that usually stuck out from her head like wires. Her big eyes were a beautiful brown under long curly eyelashes. But it was her smile that won everyone's heart. Her face would light up with such ease and happiness that she made everyone around her smile back.

Rachel was very petite, much like her mother. Her dark brown hair was soft and usually pulled back in long ringlets that hung down her back. Her eyes were dark blue and sparkled with a hint of mischief. Her nose was speckled with tiny freckles, and there was a dimple on her cheek when she smiled which was most all of the time.

The two girls played together every chance they got, but there were few places in which they could do so. Lizbet was not allowed to come into any rooms of the main house except the kitchen, unless she was doing a job in one of the rooms. Sometimes Rachel would sit with Lily and Lizbet in the kitchen while they prepared food. She would play with Lizbet in the washhouse out back while Lily washed the linens and clothes. On pretty days they would often run in the fields and pastures or play a game of tag in the huge front yard. But most of the time,

the two sat on the big back porch and read books. Rachel loved to read, and Lizbet loved to listen.

Just then, the familiar sound of shoes tromping across the wooden planks of the porch startled the girls. It was Lily, and she was after them.

"I knows da' good Lawd gave you two good ears," she scolded. "It's up to you to see dat dey works."

Lily was standing over the girls with hands on hips, staring hard at Rachel. Both girls looked up innocently.

"I knows you heard yo' mama callin' you," she pointed a long, bony finger at Rachel. "You's best get yo'self in dat house an' sat down fo' dinnuh."

Then she looked at Lizbet.

"An' you's best get yo'self to da' pump an' get us mo' watuh."

Rachel closed the Bible, and both girls stood up. They knew it was best not to say anything back to Lily but to obey quietly. Rachel gave Lizbet a look to say 'I'll meet you back here after I eat,' and the two went their separate ways.

"Is Bud back yet?" Rachel asked Lily in her most polite voice.

Lily opened the big backdoor to let Rachel step in. "No, he not back yet. But it don't mattuh none. Missuh William ready to eat. He ti'ed of waitin'."

Lily held the door patiently until Rachel was securely inside the house. She closed the door and followed Rachel down the hall, close on the little girl's heels to keep her moving in the right direction. Lily was thin, like her daughter, but not so very tall. Her hands were rough, and

her arms were bony, but she was as strong as a bull and worked harder than any woman twice her size. She kept her head wrapped in the same tight kerchief as Lizbet, and her eyes were so dark brown they looked black. It was these eyes that could bore a hole in little girls who did not mind, and Lizbet and Rachel rarely crossed her.

Lily always said that Lizbet got her size from her father, a man Lizbet nor Rachel had ever seen. According to Lily Lizbet's father was a big man, six foot four with arms and legs the size of watermelons. He had slipped away just after Lizbet was born. Lily wasn't sure why he had run away.

"Missuh William never beat him or nothin' like dat," Lily had told them once. "He jus' had a pow'ful strong spirit inside him dat made him want to roam."

When Lizbet and Rachel had asked where he was, Lily had just shrugged her shoulders and said, "Could be up No'th somewheres, could be out West, could be gobbled up by a bear somewheres in da woods, only th' good Lawd knows. Don't 'spect he'll evuh show up here agin."

Then Lily had gotten really quiet, staring out the window. Lizbet and Rachel never asked about him again.

"Ra-a-chel," Mama called again from the dining room. "Where is that girl?"

Mama and her big skirt came gliding around the door frame into the hall, nearly running over Rachel and Lily who were hurrying down the hall toward her.

"Oh!" Mama said, jumping back and catching her breath. Her hoop skirt swung out and back like a bell.

"There you are. Come, come now. Sit down. We've waited long enough."

Rachel now felt guilty for having ignored her mother. Tiptoeing to her place at the long dining table, she slid into her chair then stole a glance at her father. To her surprise he smiled. She smiled back, relieved that she was not in trouble, at least not with Papa. Picking up her fork, she prepared to stab a piece of sweet potato.

"Rachel," her mother said in her sweet but stern voice. "Your napkin, dear." Her head nodded toward the folded white cloth that lay beside Rachel's plate then nodded at Rachel.

"Oh, sorry, Mama," Rachel said softly, lowering her eyes to show remorse. But to herself she was thinking, "So many rules, why are there so many rules?" And this made her think of her older brother who seemed to live by no rules at all.

"Where's Bud?" she asked, looking at the empty chair beside her.

"He's not come back from escorting Miss Wade home from church services," replied Papa. "He may have been detained."

"He may never get away from her at all the way she clutches at him," Rachel snickered.

"Rachel," her mother scolded, "shame on you. Suzanna Wade is a very well-bred young lady who happens to be fond of your brother."

Rachel smiled and stifled a giggle. Fond was not the word for Suzanna Wade. She was madly in love with Rachel's brother, and it showed. But she was not alone. Nearly all the teenaged girls in the county were smitten with Bud. He was tall and trim, like Papa, with dark, wavy hair and the same dark blue eyes that sparkled with mischief as Rachel's. His nose, mouth, and chin were small, like Mama's, but not too delicate for a man. All in all he was a very handsome fellow.

Bud had just turned eighteen last month and was as hot-blooded and wild as a boy that age can be. Four terms of military academy had disciplined him somewhat but had not extinguished the fire that seemed to burn inside him all the time. Rachel felt it totally unjust that her brother was never bothered with rules at all while she was penned down by them from all sides. This infuriated her to no end. But, she adored Bud, and he adored his little sister.

"Let's say the blessing," interrupted Papa, just in time to spare Rachel from another one of her mother's speeches about the 'do's and don'ts' of well-bred young ladies.

Rachel lowered her head, but just before doing so, she caught a quick look between her parents. Their eyes met, and they both smiled ever so slightly. It was a strange smile, as if there was a secret only the two of them knew. Rachel had never seen her mother and father look at each other like that before, and it puzzled her. Maybe they were remembering the past, thinking of their youth, their courtship, the passion of young love. While her parents bowed their heads Rachel stared at a portrait of them on

the wall, a young bride and groom. As Papa droned out their many blessings, Rachel thought about the young couple in the portrait.

Her parents had made a handsome pair when they got married. At twenty Papa was tall and lean with dark hair and blue eyes, the features he had passed down to his son and daughter. Mama was simply beautiful at seventeen. Her dark brown hair was parted in the middle and pulled back over her ears, framing the pretty features of her face, the green eyes, the small nose, the perfectly shaped mouth. Everything about her was small and delicate, but the way she tilted her head and squared her shoulders gave off an air of pride and confidence.

Papa said amen, and Rachel's eyes left the portrait and turned to study her parents while they prepared to eat. Her father still looked very much like the younger man in the portrait, except for a more furrowed brow and a thick, black beard and moustache which were always trimmed short and neat. Her mother was still beautiful, the older green eyes even prettier, Rachel thought, and the features of her face more defined.

Rachel sighed. They must have been very much in love, not googly-eyed like Suzanna Wade and the other silly-nillies, but deeply, quietly in love. It all seemed strange to her. Maybe one day she would understand, but right now her stomach was bringing her back to reality.

Rachel took a bite and then suddenly stopped and looked around. How strange to see all the empty chairs! She couldn't remember the last time she had Sunday

dinner with just her small family. For weeks, no months, there had been a constant flow of guests at their table. And the conversation was always the same... secession... secession... secession.

Ever since South Carolina had made the big step to secede from the Union right before Christmas, there had been a big hullabaloo everywhere. Rachel knew her father was an important man in their county, maybe even in the whole state. He had served in the legislature some years back, and other important men from all over had been flocking to their house to talk with him about these things. Even Senator Jefferson Davis, or rather ex-senator since their own state of Mississippi had seceded in January, had paid her father a visit in February, right before he was made president of the Confederate States of America.

Rachel had liked President Davis right away. Even though the features of his face were sharp, the pointed chin, chiseled nose, and square jaw, his eyes were gray and very soft. He was a solemn man and appeared to be serious all the time. But he had knelt down, eye-to-eye with Rachel, and chatted with her in a most casual way. He was the father of three small children, and his tender heart easily showed. Rachel figured he didn't smile much because he had so many serious things on his mind. She was glad he was the president of their new nation.

There was a lot about secession that Rachel didn't understand. She couldn't see why everyone was getting so upset about it. She didn't know why people were saying the word 'war.' So what if the southern states wanted to make

a new nation. Why couldn't they just do it? Why didn't they have the right to make their own laws? And what was so wrong with wanting to keep their slaves? Anyone with half-sense knew that you couldn't run a plantation without slaves. And without the plantations slaves wouldn't have a place to live or work. They wouldn't have anyone to take care of them.

All this talk of war scared Rachel. Her father's friends talked as if there could be no Confederate States of America without going to war. This brought a dozen questions buzzing inside Rachel's head.

"Papa," Rachel blurted out rudely. While she had been thinking, her parents had been talking quietly about something they heard in church this morning.

"Excuse you, dear," Mama reprimanded.

"Oh, sorry, Mama," Rachel had forgotten her manners again. "Excuse me, but Papa..."

"Yes, dear," her father smiled, excusing her for the rudeness.

"Papa, I was thinkin'," Rachel began. "Why doesn't Mr. Lincoln just say goodbye to all the southern states and let everybody be happy?"

Papa chuckled. He wiped his mouth with his napkin and answered.

"Oh, to be that easy would be a miracle," Papa shook his head. "If it could only be that easy."

"But why not?" Rachel persisted, as a ten-year-old is prone to do.

Papa looked at his daughter. His smile disappeared, and he pondered the question awhile before answering again.

"For years we've been bound together as a union," he finally said, "all states together. But we no longer live the same way. We don't agree about the way people should be governed, and when the government becomes too oppressive, as ours has done, we have to stand up for our rights. The states that have seceded have done so because the people of those states believe their rights have been taken from them. And sometimes people have to fight for their rights."

"But why do we have to fight?" Rachel wanted to know. "Why can't we just say we want a new nation and do it?"

"Because the other states believe we should stay united," Papa replied. "Mr. Lincoln believes it is his job to keep the Union together, under one government, and one set of laws. And the people of the Union are willing to fight to keep it so."

"Does that mean we are going to have a war?" she asked, not really knowing what it meant to 'have a war.'

Papa sighed and looked at Mama. But before he could get out his answer, a loud commotion arose in the front yard—the beating of horses' hooves, a crack of a pistol, loud whoops that sounded like a pack of wolves—and it was growing louder by the minute.

Papa sprang from his chair and, in two giant steps, was across the room and at the front door. Mama stood up quickly and held out her hand to Rachel who skittered around the big table to clutch her mother's hand. Papa flung the door open, and they heard a familiar voice.

"It's begun!" Bud yelled, then threw back his head and whooped again. "Ya-a-a-hoo-oo-oo! The war's on. We're gonna whup some Yankees!"

There were two other boys on horseback with Bud. All three of their horses were wild-eyed from the excitement. Their nostrils were flaring as they panted hard. There were patches of white lather around the bridles and saddles where they had run fast and hard. They stomped in anticipation of taking off again.

One of the boys was Robert Yancey whose father was a well-to-do planter and close friend of the family. Robert and Bud had been lifelong friends and had even gone to military school together. The other one was Tom Harrison, another long-time friend, but whose father was not so wealthy. Tom's father was considered a farmer rather than a planter because he, Tom, and his five brothers did most of the hard labor. Tom had not gone to the academy, but he had stayed good friends with Bud and Robert. They always got together when the boys came home, and the three of them could stir up more trouble than a cyclone in a henhouse.

Right now, there was more whoopin' and hollerin' coming from those three than a whole tribe of Indians on the warpath. Papa just stood at the door watching the spectacle. One hand had fallen from the door to his side, and the other had grabbed the door frame as if he

might fall to his knees any moment. The look on his face certainly did not reflect the looks of ecstasy on the faces of the young men. Mama slid quickly to Papa's side, dragging Rachel along by the hand. She put her other hand gently on Papa's shoulder and looked up into his face. Her eyes were searching his for some kind of answer, and Rachel saw tears begin to well up in them. Rachel did not know what to make of it all, whether she should cry with her mother or shout for joy with her brother.

Just then, Bud jumped down from his prancing horse. He pulled the reins over the head of the excited animal and tied them to the hitching post. He waved to his two friends to go on without him. He knew he needed to talk to his father. The two remaining messengers spun their horses around and took off in a cloud of dust, yelling so loudly they could be heard for a good mile or more.

Bud slapped at his dusty pants as he climbed the steps and strode across the wide front porch. His dark hair was loose and wind-blown, and he tried to comb it back with his fingers. With his friends out of sight he had calmed down considerably. The looks of shock on the faces of his family huddled together in the doorway put a stop to all the yelling, and he approached them quietly. But his breathing was quick, and his eyes were still flashing with the excitement that filled his soul. Rachel stared at this madman who was supposed to be her brother and wondered if they would let him in the house.

Papa was silent. Mama spoke up in a soft but strained voice.

"Come in, Bud, sit down. You haven't had a bite to eat since breakfast."

They all went into the dining room and took their places at the table as if nothing had happened. Lily appeared out of nowhere with a plate of hot food for Bud. Her eyes were wide, darting from one face to the other, and her hand was shaking as she laid down the plate. Lily was no different from the rest of them. She wanted answers, too. She wanted to know what was going to happen. But she didn't dare say a word or intrude in any way on the family, so she lowered her eyes and scurried quietly out of the room. Rachel knew that Lily's ears would not be out of listening range.

Bud was the only one with an appetite now. They all watched as he took several bites and washed it down with a large gulp of milk. Papa put his elbows on the table, grasped his hands together, and rested his forehead on his knuckles. Rachel didn't know if he was thinking, or waiting for Bud to finish eating, or maybe praying really, really hard. But the silence didn't last long.

Papa finally dropped his hands and looked hard at Bud.

"Well, son," he began, "it was the fort, wasn't it?"

"What fort?" Mama wanted to know. She tried to look calm for her children's benefit, but her voice trembled when she spoke. In her lap she was wringing a small handkerchief unmercifully with her hands. She looked anxiously from husband to son, son to husband.

"Fort Sumter, dear," he answered; then he turned back to Bud. "Tell us what happened."

That was like pulling one's finger out of a leak in the dike. Bud's words came pouring out, without so much as taking a breath in between, and it was hard for Rachel to keep up with what he was saying.

"It was, Papa," he nodded. "The Union refused to give it up. After all that talk... makin' promises... lettin' us think they were evacuatin'... no supplies left... ready to hand it over. Then what does that ape-man Lincoln do?" Bud looked at his mother apologetically for the name-calling. She was glued to his every word and had not noticed.

"He sends a ship... right under the noses of every good citizen of Charleston... all loaded down... to re-supply the fort," Bud was shaking his head in disbelief, trying to be serious, but he couldn't control the smile that kept creeping on his face. Inside, he was overjoyed to be finally in the fight after so many months of talk about it.

Papa nodded. "I received a telegram about this just last week. It was sent by one of the commissioners from Charleston." Papa was talking mainly to Mama, trying to explain things for her. "There was great hope that the fort would not be re-supplied, that the soldiers occupying the fort would pack up and leave it to South Carolina without a shot. I was praying that it could be handed over peacefully."

"Well, it wasn't," Bud blurted out, ready to finish his story. "The Yankees wouldn't budge, and when Beauregard, General P.G.T. Beauregard, that is," Bud emphasized every initial of the revered name so his

mother would be duly impressed, "when he caught sight of that Yankee ship pulling into the harbor, he knew it was time for action. Reports say it was about 4:30 on Friday morning when the guns began to fire. And they blasted that fort all day and night." Bud was waving his fork now. "Yankees blasted right back. People say it was some show to watch. Sometime in the wee hours of Saturday morning, the fort was surrendered."

Bud looked eagerly at his father, his eyes flashing even more fiercely. He banged his fist on the table, startling Rachel and Mama, and rose out of his seat.

"The war's on."

He banged his fist again, making them jump a second time. Bud was wild with excitement.

"Let us at those Yankee boys. We'll have all of 'em... the whole stinkin' bunch of 'em... licked in no time."

In his excitement Bud had forgotten where he was and to whom he was talking. He caught his breath and took a good look at the faces around the table, Papa's somber, almost death-like look, Rachel's frightened little face, and Mama, poor Mama, about to break down in tears.

Bud sat down again and rubbed his face. He took a deep breath and waited for his father to speak. They all waited for what seemed like hours.

Finally Papa spoke.

"Bud..." he said softly, shaking his head. "War is a terrible thing... terrible." He looked down at his hands as if he alone had caused the war to happen. "I've prayed it wouldn't come to this. But it was inevitable, I suppose."

23

He looked up, realizing the effect his words were having on his wife and young daughter. Rachel's eyes showed how scared and confused she was. There was a tear on Mama's cheek. Papa reached over and put his hand on top of Mama's to comfort her. They both knew their son would be going to war, and it was breaking Mama's heart. Her back stiffened, and her face tightened as she tried to keep from breaking down.

Papa smiled at Rachel and tried to reassure her. "Everything's going to be fine, just fine. Soon things will be back as they were."

"Papa's right," Bud agreed. He leaned over putting his face close to Rachel's, grinned, and gave her a tweak on the nose. "This war won't last long." He looked across the table at Mama. "We'll have us a few good fights. Those Yanks'll be runnin' back up North before the summer's out. You'll see."

Mama was not convinced. Papa smiled and nodded, patting her hand gently. But his eyes revealed that he was not convinced either. For a few minutes the family sat in silence.

Then Bud cleared his throat. His smile suddenly disappeared, and his eyes looked at each one at the table. He was trying to find the courage to say what was coming next.

"There's a group of us," Bud cleared his throat again, now focusing his eyes on the fork he was holding. He could not bear to look his mother in the eyes as he spoke. "We're headin' up to Jackson to enlist."

"When?" Mama broke in quickly.

"Tomorrow," Bud let out a big sigh and looked up at Mama. There, he had said it. Then he looked at Papa. "Early... at dawn."

Papa just nodded his head.

Rachel was incredulous. Why didn't Papa protest? Why didn't Mama cry and insist that Bud not go? What was wrong with everybody? He shouldn't be allowed to go off to war. Somebody should stop him. Rachel was just about to burst into tears and pound her brother with her fists until he came to his senses when another big commotion occurred outside.

Everyone froze and listened. Then Papa and Bud jumped up and dashed to the front door. There was the sound of horses' hooves again, but this time there was also the sound of a buggy, no, two, maybe three buggies approaching the house. Mama and Rachel ran to the window and pulled back the tall, heavy drapes that hung in the dining room.

They saw a small, black buggy coming to a halt in front of their house. A cloud of dust churned up around the passengers inside. A lady was coughing and waving a lace handkerchief in front of her face while the driver secured the reins and climbed down from the seat. The man was short and portly, his stomach being as wide around his middle as a wagon wheel, but he was well-dressed with a black top hat and cane. It was Dr. Prentiss, and the person sitting on the buggy seat, choking on the dust, was his wife, Rosalee Prentiss. 'Miss Rosalee' was what most people called her. Rachel held her breath as

the doctor raised his hand to help his wife down from the buggy. Miss Rosalee was the biggest woman Rachel knew, and it was no easy task for her to climb in or out of a buggy. One slip and poor Dr. Prentiss could be crushed beneath her.

A second buggy pulled up beside the Prentiss's, and Rachel could see, in spite of the dust that had been stirred up, that this one contained Mr. and Mrs. Millbrook, good friends of her parents. Rachel smiled. She was glad the Millbrooks had come to call because they were younger than her parents and always full of laughter, especially Mrs. Millbrook who was not only fun but very pretty, too. They had no children yet, and she was always attentive to Rachel, helping her with needlework or reading to her from one of her poetry books. It was always a delight to be with Mrs. Millbrook.

There were also two men on horseback. Rachel did not know their names but recognized them as two of the many visitors who had come to their house in the last few months. They jumped down from their horses very quickly as a third wagon pulled up alongside carrying two more men. There was such excitement in the air that Rachel felt as though they were having one of their big galas instead of a war.

Mama felt it, too. She quickly forgot about Bud and the war and tears. She had guests, and this meant she had to spring into action as their hostess.

"Rachel, quick dear," she ordered, "go tell Lily to clear the dining table. Tell her to prepare tea and cakes and

bring them to the parlor. There's no time to waste."

Rachel scooted down the long hall and toward the kitchen as quickly as she could. She found Lily peeking out the door to see what was going on, but when Lily saw Rachel she immediately ducked out of sight and closed the door. Lily wouldn't dare be caught eavesdropping. That was a punishable crime for a slave, especially a house slave. But her curiosity about all this excitement was almost more than she could stand. All work ceased, and all eyes stared at Rachel when she rushed into the kitchen.

This startled Rachel somewhat, but she quickly caught her breath and delivered Mama's message to Lily. And as soon as she did Lily began giving orders of her own. There were two other house girls besides Lily and Lizbet. Rachel knew their names were Jo and Mott, although she had never spoken to them nor had they ever even looked at Rachel. Lily sent them hurrying out of the room to clear away the family's dinner that had hardly been touched. Then she snapped instructions to Lizbet as she hustled about herself grabbing pots and trays and bowls.

"Lawsy me!" she exclaimed. "Dey's sum'pin not right. It just ain't right all dis 'motion."

Lily was used to having guests at the house, very often, for dinner and parties, but not all these uninvited people coming in such a flurry of noise. Lily and Lizbet both eyed Rachel. They wanted to know what was going on but didn't dare ask. Rachel, on the other hand, was bursting to tell.

"It's the war!" Rachel cried. "We're havin' a war."

"Here?" asked Lizbet with eyes about ready to pop out of her head. "In dis house?"

"No, don't be silly," Rachel frowned. "Not here. Somewhere off. You have to go off to war."

Rachel didn't know much about all this war stuff, but she certainly knew more than her two listeners. They were eager for her to explain. So Rachel settled herself in an old cane-backed chair and talked while the other two worked.

"You see," Rachel began. "There was this fort. And the people in it," Rachel looked at Lizbet who was listening intently, "they're called Yankees."

A puzzled look came across Lizbet's face. Rachel continued to explain.

"Yankees, 'cause they're from up North... well, the Yankees didn't have any food in this fort, and when the ship tried to bring them food it made Mr. Beau... Mr. G.P.... Beau... well, some man real mad. And he started shootin' at the fort until the people, the Yankees, came out."

By the looks on their faces neither mother nor daughter understood what Rachel was saying, but they kept listening while their hands stayed busy.

"And now we're havin' a war," Rachel stated rather simply. "But that's not the whole reason we're havin' a war. It has to do with rights and secession and Mr. Lincoln not lettin' the people in the South do what they want to do."

Rachel's face saddened as she thought of Bud.

"And now Bud's got to go enlist," she added. "He wants to go fight the Yankees, and Papa's not even gonna stop him."

28

"Can't stop 'im," Lily said flatly as she stirred a bowl of flour, eggs, milk, and sugar. "He got to go fight de Yankees. Can't have Yankees trompin' on our land, takin' ovuh our home." She looked up at Rachel while she kept stirring. "Now, can we?"

Rachel frowned in frustration. No one understood that her brother should not go off to war. Bud could just as well stay home and protect his family from the Yankees right here.

In the blink of an eye and the twist of a hand Lily had whipped up a pan of tea cakes. She handed the pan to Lizbet and sent her hurrying out the backdoor to the little building that housed the wood-burning stove. Rachel jumped up to follow her friend, but, quick as lightning, Lily snatched her by the sash. Lily had a way of grabbing onto a sash so quickly and tightly that it felt like one more step could split a little girl in half at the waist. Rachel stopped dead in her tracks.

"You get yo'self back to Miss Belle," Lily was referring to Rachel's mother. "Go see does she needs you."

Lily was right. Rachel needed to get back to Mama. Besides, she wanted to see Mrs. Millbrook, so she hurried to the kitchen door. Just as she reached it the door swung open, and she nearly collided with Jo and Mott who were returning with the family's dinner dishes. Neither girl spoke nor even looked at Rachel. They kept their heads lowered and clutched their precious stacks of china. Rachel excused herself for the near accident, slipped past them carefully, and hurried down the hall.

By now all the unexpected guests had moved inside the house, and all formalities of welcoming finished. Papa was directing the male visitors into the dining room, and to Rachel's surprise, he pulled together the tall sliding doors that were never used to separate this room from the hallway, sealing it off from the rest of the house.

Mama was helping her two female guests with their shawls as Miss Rosalee chittered like an excited bird. "Our poor brave boys... going off to war... oh, dear me... so much to be done... must have a committee." She waved her handkerchief as she flittered and chirped. Mama simply nodded and smiled as she guided the two ladies into the parlor and offered them a comfortable place to sit. Then Mama caught sight of Rachel and motioned for her to come in. Rachel knew that her manners were being scrutinized closely by her mother, so she put on her sweetest smile and tried her best to be very ladylike. Miss Rosalee 'oohed' over how much she had grown and 'aahed' over how pretty she was becoming. "Pretty like her mother, but my, she does have her father's eyes, Belle."

Rachel sat on the loveseat next to young Mrs. Millbrook. Laura was her first name (Miss Laura to Rachel), and Rachel thought she was almost as pretty as her mother. She had golden blonde hair that was pulled back in a bun at her neck. Her eyes were blue, and she had a beautiful smile, a smile she was sharing with Rachel just now as Miss Rosalee chattered on, not letting anyone else get a word in edgewise.

"We must get word to all the ladies," she was saying. "We need to organize a sewing group, and there's money to be raised, oh, my, there's a great deal to do."

"Yes, no doubt," Mama answered calmly. "We'll need committees, I'm sure." Then Mama looked across the room at Miss Laura. They both had the same teary-eyed look as they tried to smile at each other. Miss Laura spoke first.

"Evan's going to enlist tomorrow," she said, her voice quivering with emotion. Mama jumped up quickly, rustled across the room, and sat down in the small space between Miss Laura and Rachel, nearly sitting on top of her daughter. Rachel tried to free herself as she pulled at her skirt and wiggled out from under her mother's bigger skirt.

"I know, dear," Mama comforted. "Bud's going, too."

She placed one hand on Miss Laura's shoulder and patted her hand with the other. Both had pretty lace handkerchiefs that they now used to dab their eyes.

"Of course they're enlisting," Miss Rosalee broke in, rather gruffly. There was business to take care of, and this sniveling was wasting time. "This is a glorious day, a glorious war. You wouldn't want your brave, young men sitting at home while there's a war to fight. They must defend their homes and their families... and their rights."

Miss Rosalee's white handkerchief was waving again like a flag in a windstorm. She had worked herself up with her own enthusiasm, but her words had a calming effect on the other two women. They knew in their hearts that she was right. Husbands and sons of women all over the

South would be leaving their homes to fight this war. It would not be easy for any of them.

Mama turned to look into Miss Laura's face.

"Will you be all right?" she asked fretfully. "Is there someone who can take care of you when... when it's time..." She glanced around nervously at Rachel and across the room at Miss Rosalee.

Miss Laura broke in. "Yes, I'm going to my in-laws to stay."

Then, she glanced around at the others, too, and added, "It's all right." She blushed and lowered her eyes. The two women smiled at each other and clasped hands. Rachel wondered why her mother and Miss Laura were acting so strangely.

"We're expecting," Miss Laura looked at Rachel and Miss Rosalee and smiled. It was the most beautiful smile Rachel had ever seen. It took a few seconds for Rachel to grasp what she had said, but suddenly Rachel's mouth popped open and her eyes got big.

"A baby?" she cried. "Do you mean a baby?"

Everyone laughed. The room was suddenly filled with that joy and warmth that comes from women when they think and talk about babies. It is an excitement like no other.

"When's it comin'?" Rachel asked, bubbling over from the news.

Miss Laura blushed again, "Well, he... or she," she looked around at the smiling faces and laughed, "should be here in late November."

This time when Miss Laura smiled, Rachel thought she absolutely glowed.

"Well, there you have it," Miss Rosalee flipped her handkerchief at the three ladies huddled on the love seat together. "Evan'll be back before the baby comes. You mark my words. Our brave boys will give those Yankees such a fight, they'll be back up North and ready to settle this matter from behind their desks."

Just then, one of the house girls, whether it was Jo or Mott was hard to say because the girl never looked up, appeared at the threshold of the parlor. She was holding a tray loaded down with a steaming teapot, four delicately painted tea cups and saucers, and a plate of cakes that had just been removed from the hot oven. Steam rose from the cakes and carried their aroma throughout the room. Rachel realized she had not had a sufficient meal, and she was ravenous. But she knew that good manners went before growling stomachs, and she would have to wait until their guests were served before having anything herself. Mama would be mortified if the rules of etiquette were broken. And Rachel knew her mother was a gracious hostess. She would take her time and serve each one slowly and in small portions, so as not to appear too 'piggish.'

Rachel felt as though she could eat the whole plate of cakes in one bite, but she would be forced to eat a very small one in tiny nibbles. Ladies were not supposed to have big appetites, and they were to act like eating was just a form of leisure rather than a necessity. Rachel eyed Miss Rosalee's chubby fingers delicately picking up a cake and giggled to herself. She knew Miss Rosalee hadn't acquired such a 'full figure' by taking nibbles.

As the ladies sipped on tea and nibbled on cake, the atmosphere in the room had become lighter, almost gay. News of the baby had lightened everyone's spirits, and now they could discuss the festive events that would accompany their men marching off to war. Rachel only half-listened as they organized sewing groups and planned benefit balls. She was more interested in sneaking a second cake without Mama noticing. But, when talk shifted to the flag-waving ceremonies and rallies with fiery speeches to spur heroic men to battle, she perked up and listened. She began to catch the enthusiasm that was in the air. She thought of how anxious her brother was to go and fight the Yankees. How grand it must feel to ride off to war! Such honor, such bravery, such adventure! She was almost jealous of him getting to leave for the war while she had to stay at home and fumble with a needle and thread. She envisioned a great send-off: people cheering, bands playing, hats waving, handkerchiefs fluttering. She could picture Bud, so handsome in his uniform atop his horse, waving and then bending down to kiss all the girls goodbye. It was a good daydream but not at all reality.

The next morning when Bud prepared to leave there were no bands playing, no people cheering, no flags waving. The sun was not yet up, and it was dark and cold. A light drizzle of rain added to the dreariness that surrounded everything. Bud and Rachel had said their good-byes the night before. Rachel was not normally up before dawn, and Bud insisted that she not see him off at this hour. But her mind knew what was happening and would not let her sleep. She woke up and jumped from the bed as Bud was outside packing his gear onto his horse.

Rachel pressed her forehead against her bedroom window on the second floor and watched the shadowy outlines of people moving below. They were working by the light of a lantern, and it was hard to make out who was there. But Rachel knew the tall man was their father and a smaller man, besides Bud, must be old Josup. Bud was pulling at straps and tying down bundles that hung off his horse.

She watched as Bud said his farewell, hugging Papa in a long bear hug, patting each other's backs as men do. Then a small figure appeared from out of the darkness and clasped Bud around the neck. They embraced a long time. Rachel knew it was Mama, and like the raindrops that were rolling down her window, tears began rolling down Rachel's cheeks. Her heart beat quickly as she saw Bud turn and put his foot in the stirrup. She wanted to run down the stairs and scream for him to stop. She wanted to hug him once more, but there wasn't time. He would be gone before she could make it to him.

Dawn was just beginning to break, bringing a faint light to the darkness. Rachel could see Bud swing his leg over the large bundle he had tied behind his saddle. Her heart pounded, and her breathing came so fast she felt as

if she could not breathe at all. He couldn't leave; he just couldn't. She had to say goodbye.

In her panic, Rachel began beating on the window. She was yelling Bud's name, trying to be heard above the rain and the horse. She beat on the glass furiously, as Bud pulled the reins and dug his heels into the flanks of the sleepy horse, urging him forward. Then, with her face and her open palms pressed hard against the window, she sobbed as he passed beneath her. Just when she thought he was gone forever, Bud stopped his horse and looked up. In the dim light she could barely see his face, but she knew he was smiling. He waved to her, then reached into his coat pocket and pulled out the small piece of ribbon she had given him last night. He raised it toward her then tucked it safely back into his pocket. He touched his cap in a sort of farewell salute. Then, with a flick of his wrist, he galloped away.

Bud was off to fight the Yankees.

Rachel remembered what Mama had told her last night. She said that men were not the only ones who had to be brave. It was their job to be brave as well. Neither Mama nor Rachel knew then just how brave they would have to be in the coming days.

For, by May's end, Papa would be off to war, too.

3

The Ones Left Behind

may, 1861

OUCH! RACHEL PUT HER FINGER TO HER LIPS. She had pricked her finger again, and it was very sore. Miss Rosalee had been right. There was a great deal to be done, and ever since that day when Bud had come whooping down the lane to tell them about the start of the war, the world seemed like one gigantic beehive. Rachel had been thinking about a beehive that Lizbet and she had once found when she accidentally let the needle slip into her finger. She was remembering how loudly the bees had buzzed as they swarmed around the hive working furiously at whatever it was they were doing. The two girls had watched in fascination. Now, people everywhere were buzzing and swarming, just like bees, making this and gathering that, so busy, busy, busy.

In the past few weeks there had been no end of guests at their house. Some were couriers with telegrams, some were messengers, others were old friends wanting to talk about the war or organizing groups to raise money and troops and all the thousand-and-one necessary things needed right now. There was lots of news about the armies that were being formed, mainly state militias, whose numbers were growing every day. It seemed like all the men and boys in Mississippi had left home to fight in the war.

But, when Papa slipped away to join the other men at war, the excitement left with him. Frantic men on horseback who jumped from their saddles to bring Papa important messages no longer came. Late night meetings behind the closed doors of the dining room had stopped. Papa had been gone only six days, but Rachel missed him terribly, and it felt like he had been away for weeks. The sudden lull of activity made matters even worse. It seemed to Rachel that everybody had plunged into the adventure of war, but she was left at home to sew. Rachel stared at the needle and thread in her hands with disgust. She knew Papa would want her to help in this way, but it didn't make her feel any better. As she thought about Papa, her mind drifted to the night he left and their last moments together.

Papa had sat on her bed, not saying a word as the old clock in the hall ticked the minutes away. Rachel remembered the sick feeling that had come over her as she waited

for her father to speak. She knew something was wrong but was afraid to hear what Papa might tell her. He patted her hands and brushed back the loose curls that lay around her neck. There was such a sad look in Papa's eyes that Rachel believed Bud must be dead. Her heart began to pound, and just as she started to cry out, Papa took a deep breath and said,

"Rachel... sweetheart... I'm going to be leaving."

Rachel had sat up quickly and searched her father's face.

"Oh, no, Papa!" she cried. "Not the war. You can't go off to the war, too."

"Hush now, dear," he had tried to soothe her. "I have to go. I'm needed there. I... I have no other choice."

Rachel remembered putting her hands to her face and sobbing. Papa had tried to comfort her by pressing her head to his chest and rocking her gently like a baby. She had listened to the steady beat of his heart and felt the warmth of his arms around her.

"I wish that I could stay here and take care of you and your mother," he had said softly. "But our army needs men... not only men to be soldiers, but men to be leaders. President Davis has asked me to be one of those leaders."

"But... " Rachel sniffed. "But... why you, Papa?"

"Because I was once a soldier," he had explained. "A long time ago, when I was much younger, I was a soldier under Mr. Davis. We fought in a war with Mexico. We've known each other a long time, and he thinks that I can help."

Then Papa had taken Rachel by the shoulders, pulled her upright, and looked squarely into her tear-stained face.

"There are thousands of boys, just like our Bud, who have left their homes to fight for this new nation," Papa's blue eyes were moist, and his soft voice trembled. "They need good leaders... and they need help. It may take every good man in the South to get us through this war."

Papa had kissed Rachel on the head as she sobbed again.

"But, Papa... who'll take care of us?"

"Y'all have Lily and Josup... and the others," he had said. "They'll keep everything in order. I've stayed until the crops were planted, and Mr. Gunther can take care of them now."

Rachel thought of Mr. Gunther. He had been the overseer for as long as she could remember. He was not so tall as Papa but stout as a bull with big, muscular arms and legs that were covered with freckles and tiny, curly red hairs. His thick hair was also red and curly, and his face looked like that of a sow's, big jowls and large nose. It was always red, like he had just scrubbed it raw with lye soap. One of his eyes had been injured in an accident, and Rachel thought it was scary to look at the clouded eye that didn't look back. He spoke in half-English, half-German words with so thick an accent that it was almost impossible to understand him. His hands and arms were always moving in gestures to get his message across.

Although he clearly pronounced his own name as 'Goon-ter' everyone still called him Gunther. His wife's

name was Elsa (which he pronounced Elt-za), and they lived in a small house past the slave quarters near the bayou. They had three sons, two of whom were grown and had taken off on their own some years back. Their youngest boy was named Henrich, which naturally became Henry to everyone except his parents. He was only thirteen, and even though he was rather scrawny for his age, he was required to do the work of an adult to help out. Rachel thought it was little wonder that the older two boys had run away from such back-breaking hard labor, and she guessed Henry would do the same in a few more years.

Rachel rarely saw Mr. Gunther, his wife Elsa, or Henry, and she was glad. She didn't like Henry because he didn't like her. He was quick to show his dislike with hateful looks and spiteful remarks that he whispered at her between his teeth so no one else would hear. Rachel was afraid of this strange German family, and the thought of being in Mr. Gunther's care made her shiver. Rachel would much rather Mr. Gunther go to war and Papa stay home to watch the crops. But, she knew that was impossible, and Papa trusted Mr. Gunther to take care of them. She would just have to trust him, too.

Ouch! Rachel's daydream was broken by another prick of the needle. She shook her finger and examined it closely then glanced across the parlor to see if Mama was watching her. Mama was bent over her sewing with head down, seemingly absorbed in her work, but Rachel knew she was deep in thought. It was an unusual afternoon, to

be sure. Rachel and Mama were all alone, which was a rare event these days. The ladies who had come by buggy each day to plan and organize, to sew and socialize, had not appeared today. All the windows were open, and a warm breeze was blowing through the room. There was a faint smell of honeysuckle and the soft sounds of birds chirping. Mama seemed to enjoy the peace and quiet, but it allowed her mind to think about Papa and Bud and all the worries that went along with their absence. Or maybe she was thinking about the news she had just read in Bud's letter.

Bud's letters came weekly, and Rachel loved to curl up at Mama's feet to listen as she read them out loud. She had just finished the one that had arrived today. The

pages still lay open on her lap. Bud had written the same old news of rain and mud and drilling. He always put in a funny story or mentioned familiar names to amuse Rachel. But, as Mama read on, she had begun to mumble the words. She had frowned, and her voice had dropped to a whisper as she tried to read quickly.

"What is it, Mama?" Rachel wanted to know.

"Oh, sorry, dear," Mama apologized. She was still looking at the page in dismay. "It seems that Bud's professor at the academy, Colonel Sherman... you remember him, don't you?"

Rachel nodded.

"Well, it seems that Colonel Sherman has returned to his home state of Ohio." Mama's eyes moved back to the top of the page, and she read the news again, this time slowly and loudly enough for Rachel to understand.

Mama shook her head as she finished reading and dropped the letter in her lap. Of course, not everyone they knew would be fighting for The Cause. Many Southerners who had married or moved to the South would return to their homelands and fight for the North. But it was still upsetting to hear it. Colonel Sherman had been a friend of the family's ever since the Louisiana Military Academy had opened, and Bud had been one of the first students. They had visited Bud there on several occasions, and each time, Colonel Sherman had always been warm and polite. He especially seemed to enjoy dancing with Mama at one of the balls they had attended there, and he had even whirled Rachel around the dance floor, making her giggle.

Yes, she remembered Mr. Sherman. Rachel had liked him very much, although she thought he was a little strange-looking, tall, skinny, and red-bearded. His unruly hair always looked like he had just scratched his head really hard, making it stick straight up. His eyes, although not especially attractive, reflected a mind always at work. She liked his name, William Tecumseh Sherman, because she thought the Tecumseh part sounded like an Indian chief. She hated to think that he was going to be a Yankee. She hoped that he and Bud would never have to shoot at each other.

Ouch! Rachel's hand jerked away from her sewing as if it were a hot coal. In only a few minutes, she had pricked her finger a third time. She had not learned the art of moving the sharp needle without total concentration, and each time her mind drifted to other things, she paid for it.

Mama looked up with a sympathetic smile.

"Rachel, dear, why don't you put away your sewing for a while," she said in a soft voice. They were working on a flag for Bud's company, and there wasn't much time left to finish. Every hand and every minute were needed to complete the project. There was a huge rally planned in July to present flags to all the troops who would then parade past everyone in grand fashion. With all the drilling that had been going on, it should be quite a show, and Rachel was very excited.

Rachel looked at Mama in surprise. She would like nothing better than to put away her sewing, but she knew how important it was to get the job finished.

Mama could sense Rachel's hesitation and insisted, "Put it away, hon', and go ask Lily to bring me some tea."

Rachel obeyed her mother happily. She needed to stretch her legs and was relieved to be on an errand.

When Rachel entered the kitchen, everyone was busy doing different jobs, and no one seemed to notice her. Lily was sitting in an old rocker, shelling early peas and humming to herself as her fingers nimbly broke the peas from the hulls and flicked the hulls in a burlap sack by the chair. Lizbet was washing big, leafy greens in a bucket of water and placing them in an iron pot for boiling. Jo was on her hands and knees, scrubbing the wooden floor with a large, soapy brush, and Mott was polishing silverware with a white cleaning cloth. Each of them seemed to be in her own world of thought, and Rachel stood there several minutes watching before Lily finally looked up.

"What y'all needin'?" she said, her quick fingers never stopping their work.

"Mama would like some tea," Rachel answered. Lily immediately put the pan of peas on the floor and headed for the teacups. Lizbet looked up from her greens and smiled wide. Rachel smiled back. They had not played together, or even talked, for weeks.

Lily mumbled something to Lizbet while passing by her carrying a tray for the teapot. Lizbet nodded and put the last of the greens in the pot. She got up from her knees,

picked up the heavy iron pot, and headed for the backdoor. Rachel quickly moved to join her friend, keeping an eye on Lily and her quick-as-lightning hands. She expected to feel a hard yank on her sash to hold her in place, and when it didn't come, she slipped out the door quickly on the heels of her friend.

They walked in silence across the wide back porch, down the steps, and over to the outdoor spit. Rachel watched Lizbet strain as she lifted the handle of the big pot and hooked it to the metal rack that hung above the fire. Then Lizbet stoked the fire until small blazes rose up, heating the water in the pot and making it simmer. Long minutes passed as the two girls watched the water start to bubble in the pot, neither one saying a word. Finally, Lizbet broke the silence.

"When's Missuh William comin' back?"

Rachel shrugged her shoulders, still watching the pot, and mumbled, "Don't know."

Her answer seemed to satisfy Lizbet who simply nodded her head, not moving her eyes from the bubbling water. It was not unusual for fathers, like Lizbet's own father, to leave without knowing when, or if, they would return.

Rachel then looked at her friend.

"He'll be home when the war's over, I guess," she said.

"When dat be?" asked Lizbet.

"Don't know," Rachel mumbled again. "Bud says at the end of the summer."

"Da end o' da summer!" Lizbet exclaimed. "Who gonna git in da crops?" Who gonna look afta' all us all dat time?"

"Papa says Mr. Gunther'll take care of everything," said Rachel.

Lizbet's face went from wide-eyed surprise to an expressionless, blank-eyed look. Rachel had seen this look many times from the other slaves but never from Lizbet. It was a look that all slaves used when confronted by white people to hide their thoughts and emotions, to show no fear or anger, to make themselves 'invisible.' Lizbet had learned this skill from Lily who had learned it, in turn, from her father, Josup. All slaves knew how to make their faces void of expression, and Lizbet was doing it now.

"What's wrong?" Rachel wanted to know. She didn't like this stone-cold face, and she knew something was wrong with her friend. She touched Lizbet's arm. "What is it?"

Lizbet stayed quiet for a long time, looking down, as she stirred the pot of greens. Then finally she looked at Rachel with life back in her eyes.

She whispered as if he were standing right behind them. "I don't likes Missuh Gunt'er. I don't likes 'im at all. I scared of 'im."

Rachel patted Lizbet on the shoulder. She thought of how Mama comforted her friends whenever they were distressed and tried to imitate her. She bent over and looked squarely into Lizbet's down-turned face.

"I don't like him either," she tried to reassure Lizbet. "But Papa says it'll be all right, so it will. And he and Bud'll be back in a couple of months, and everything'll be just as it was before."

Lizbet's eyes still showed fear and worry as she continued to stir the bubbling pot.

"Mama says we have to be brave," Rachel remembered her mother's speech. "We have to take care of ourselves and our home. We have to do everything we can to help our brave men who are tryin' to protect us from the Yankees."

Lizbet was not convinced. But she gave a half-smile for the effort made to boost her courage. Then Lizbet's smile vanished as quickly as her courage, her lower lip protruded again in a pout, and she mumbled,

"Wish Missuh William come back now."

Rachel stood close to her friend and stared into the steaming pot. Her words had been just that, words. She, too, felt no courage, only a terrible sense of dread and loneliness and fear. Then suddenly, as if the sky were feeling the same as the two girls beneath it, small raindrops began to fall from a lone dark cloud above them. The drops came quicker and peppered the girls as they ran across the yard to the safety of the porch.

4

Kiss The Girls Goodbye

july 2, 1861

As the warm days of June steadily heated up toward the hot days of July so did the excitement and activity. Rachel soon forgot the dread she had felt on that rainy day weeks ago, and in its place was a wonderful sense of pride and anticipation. All the ladies had been working furiously on the flag that was to be presented to their troops, and it was nearly finished. Rachel was proud of her needle-pricked fingers and the part she had played in putting the masterpiece together. She was ecstatic about the festivities that were only a few days away. But, more than anything else, she could hardly wait to see her brother and father again.

The sun rose bright and hot on the second day of July. Rachel squirmed on the wagon seat as she waited for the two men named Blue and Tom to help Josup pack the supplies. Although it was still early morning, beads of sweat popped out on the brows of the dark-skinned men, and they grunted low in their chests as they heaved the large crates and bulging bags on the wagon.

It was going to be a long trip, and Rachel was anxious to get started. Mama finally emerged from the house carrying a large basket that Lily had packed with their lunches. Josup took the basket from Mama and helped her climb up onto the wagon seat. Normally, they would have ridden in the carriage. It was much more comfortable for ladies, especially in the July heat. But Papa had sent a long list of supplies that were badly needed, and the only way to bring them was in the old buckboard pulled by a pair of strong mules. So there sat Rachel on the hard wooden seat wedged between Mama and Josup with barely enough room for the three of them. Rachel twisted her skirts from under her to get more comfortable, nudging both her companions in the process. It was going to be a long trip, a very long trip.

Josup slapped the reins and, in his low, deep voice, 'Gee-ee-yupped' the mules forward. As if sensing the importance of their cargo, persons and supplies alike, the two long-eared animals stepped without hesitation. The wagon jerked forward causing Mama to grab the side rail as she settled onto the seat, squeezing Rachel tightly against Josup's thin, muscular arm. The three travelers atop the old wagon bounced and jerked as they slowly left their home in the distance. Like their men before them, the women of the Franklin family were off to do their duty for the war. Rachel felt as though she was finally getting to share in the adventure, and her heart pounded with excitement and pride.

The sun was very low in the sky when the wagon finally rumbled down the lane to its first destination, a plantation owned by Miss Laura's in-laws. Three generations had been born and raised there, and with Miss Laura's baby due in the fall, it was likely that a fourth generation would begin there as well. It would have been impossible to make Jackson, the site of the big rally, in a day, and Mama had happily accepted a gracious invitation to spend the night with the Millbrook family. Rachel was anxious to see Miss Laura again and now, as the wagon came to a halt in front of the huge columns of the beautiful mansion, she was all tingly inside with excitement.

But that wasn't the only thing that was tingly. In her haste to get down from the wagon Rachel discovered that her rump and legs had gone numb from sitting so long. And now that the blood had surged back into them, everything from the waist down was tingling, and she could barely walk. She made a face at the mule named Sam who had turned in his harness to watch her get down from the wagon and seemed to be laughing at her.

Rachel shook out her stiff legs, stomped her dead-ened feet, and hobbled to the porch steps as quickly as she could for Miss Laura had just come rushing out the

front door and was embracing Mama. The two women were absolutely bubbling over with excitement at seeing one another again, and the sight of her mother's cheerful face made Rachel forget about the long, tiresome journey and her aching body. It had been a long time since she had seen Mama smile.

Miss Laura squealed with delight as she ran to meet Rachel. Rachel could see that Miss Laura's tiny waist had rounded out, and she was careful not to wrap her arms around the expectant mother too tightly. Miss Laura had been terribly homesick for her husband and her friends, and she couldn't hide her excitement at having Mama and Rachel there. She darted back and forth between the two of them, hugging and chattering, until her mother-in-law, Mrs. Francine Millbrook, hustled them all into the house and sat them down at a long dining table loaded with delicious food.

There was roast pork and baked ham, yams, corn on the cob, black-eyed peas, cornbread and biscuits just out of the oven, and slices of juicy red tomatoes. For dessert there was pecan pie. Rachel was hungry, very hungry, and she took the first few bites without even chewing, not the best manners for a young lady. Luckily for Rachel, Mama was not paying attention to her appetite just now. She was too busy answering the hundred-and-one questions hurled at her by Miss Laura. How was dear Mrs. So-and-so, and what about the Anderson's new baby, and oh, my, did the young couple at church ever get engaged? Miss Laura was like a fountain overflowing with questions.

After only a few bites Rachel realized how very tired she was. Neither this delicious food nor being with bubbly Miss Laura Millbrook could fight off the exhaustion she was feeling. It was easy to read the fatigue on Mama's face as well, and after a short but filling meal, the older Mrs. Millbrook insisted that Mama and Rachel retire to their room. Plenty of time for all this chit-chat tomorrow. Miss Laura's face dropped with disappointment, but she knew she needed her rest, too, for the journey the next day.

As soon as her head hit the pillow, before she had a chance to say her prayers or even good-night, Rachel was fast asleep, dreaming about the big day. She dreamed of boys dressed in homemade uniforms, horses that pranced with their heads and tails arched high, and flags waving as far as the eye could see. Bud was in her dream, sitting atop his horse, looking strangely like a statue. There was Papa, too, and Rachel dreamed she was chasing the two of them, but she couldn't catch them. They both went deeper into the cheering crowd until she lost sight of them. "Papa! Papa!" Rachel was calling out desperately in her sleep until she woke herself up.

It was a wild dream, but not even in her wildest dreams could Rachel have imagined what she actually did see the next day. As the Millbrook carriage brought its passengers (Mama, Rachel, Miss Laura, Mrs. Millbrook, and Mr. Millbrook, the driver) into the city, Rachel could see rows and rows of tents and campfires covering the hillsides. Some of the tents were well-made with flaps for doors. Others looked like only a piece of canvas stretched over poles with barely enough room inside for a man to lie down. Rachel thought the strangest shelter was the one made of tree branches. Soldiers simply created an arbor in a clump of trees by connecting poles horizontally to the trees in a criss-cross pattern, then covering the poles with leafy branches. She later found out that these make-shift shelters were called 'she-bangs,' and they had been erected quickly by men who did not have their own tents for protection from the hot summer sun.

Rachel shielded her eyes from that hot sun now as she gazed in awe at the white speckles that seemed to stretch for miles in all directions. She wondered which of those tents belonged to Bud and which campfire he sat by at night to write the many letters he sent home. Rachel's mind did not have a chance to think on this very long, for things began to happen quickly and in all directions.

As the carriage drew closer to the many houses and buildings that made up the city of Jackson, there were people everywhere. Hundreds of carriages and wag-ons loaded down with people and supplies jammed the main streets. Men on horseback yelled above the noise and waved drivers in various directions. Rachel looked behind their carriage to see if Josup and the other two wagons that belonged to the Millbrooks, all packed tightly with supplies, were still there. Poor Josup, thought Rachel. All this commotion must be frightening to him. Although he sat expressionless aboard the wagon, Rachel could see his thin jaw was tight as if he were gritting his teeth, and the muscles in his arms and hands were tense as he held

the reins. He stayed close behind their carriage as they moved painstakingly slowly through the crowded street.

Rachel was overcome with excitement. She felt as if she could jump right out of her skin if she didn't see Papa or Bud soon, and she kept turning and bouncing on the carriage seat. Normally, Mama would've scolded Rachel for so much fidgeting in the presence of older Mrs. Millbrook, but Mama was overcome with excitement, too. She and Miss Laura were both fidgeting almost as much as Rachel in hopes of seeing the men they hadn't seen in so long.

There were so many men dressed as soldiers it was hard to know a familiar face if you saw one. Everyone was searching faces for loved ones, and there was an occasional call or wave from across the crowd. Suddenly, from out of the sea of horses and people, came a familiar voice.

"Belle! Over here, Belle!"

It was Papa, and he was guiding his horse carefully toward them. Mama didn't wait but jumped out of the carriage and pushed her way to him. Papa jumped down from his horse and swooped her up in his arms. Mama was crying tears of joy, and Papa was wiping them away with his handkerchief and kissing her face gently.

"Papa!" Rachel cried when she realized what had happened. "Oh, Papa!"

And she scrambled down from the slow-moving carriage, too. Afraid she might get buried in the crowd, Papa hurried to Rachel and lifted her off the ground. Rachel wrapped her arms around his neck and squeezed hard.

She had never been so thrilled to see anyone in her whole life. She wanted Papa to hold her forever and never put her down. And he didn't put her down, not on the ground anyway, but rather, sat her atop his horse as he led them back to the carriage and the two Millbrook ladies.

Miss Laura was bubbling over. "Oh, William, it's so good to see you!"

"You're looking well, William," added Mrs. Millbrook, senior.

Papa thanked the ladies and complimented them as well. He nodded in recognition to an irritable Mr. Millbrook sitting on the driver's seat who simply grunted and forced a smile. Then Papa made a few gentlemanly comments as a matter of courtesy; but, he was smiling all the while, knowing that the younger Mrs. Millbrook was about to burst to know the whereabouts of her own husband. She was trying hard to show good manners in front of her mother-in-law, but finally she could contain herself no longer.

"William, have you seen Evan?" she asked in a pleading voice. "Do you know where he is? Please can we find him?"

Papa smiled, and for the first time Rachel realized he had shaved his beard and trimmed his moustache. He suddenly looked different but very handsome, Rachel thought.

"Yes, Laura, as a matter of fact, I do know where Evan is," Papa grinned at Miss Laura and then looked at Mama. "He's with Bud, and we can go see them both now."

Miss Laura clapped her hands in sheer joy.

"In fact, we'll have to go quickly because there's not much time left before the review of troops," he added, then looked around at the jammed roadway. "It may be faster if we all walk." He looked from Mama to Miss Laura to Mrs. Millbrook and back to Miss Laura. "That is, if you think you can make it. It *is* a few blocks."

"Oh, I can make it!" exclaimed Miss Laura. "Even if it's a few *miles!*"

Papa held out his hand to help Miss Laura descend from the carriage. Mrs. Millbrook wanted to see her son badly enough, too, but she had the rheumatism and thought the walk might be too much for her. She would just have to re-unite with him after the parade. With a flick of her handkerchief and a flutter of her fan, she gave Mr. Millbrook the signal to proceed onward. Actually, there was no way to proceed *anywhere* in this jammed up street, but, like an obedient husband, he grunted to himself and flicked the reins as if to take off anyway.

Papa used the horse, with Rachel on its back, to cut a path through the throng of people. Rachel glanced back and waved goodbye to Josup. He was still expressionless, but the whites of his eyes were huge. Rachel knew he must be really terrified now as he watched them disappear. In the midst of all these people she would be frightened, too, if it weren't for the excitement of seeing Papa and Bud.

Miss Laura was first to break away as they left the crowded main streets and came to a clearing where large groups of soldiers were milling about. Somehow she had spotted her beloved husband, and her legs couldn't carry

her to him fast enough. She gathered up her long, hoop skirt and petticoats, showing her black high-top shoes and stockings, and trotted quickly into Evan's arms. Mama was appalled. She called after Miss Laura to stop. Not only was it terribly unladylike to run in public but also dangerous in her condition.

But, before Mama could fuss too much, she spotted Bud and up came her petticoats and hoop skirt as well. She took off in a more ladylike trot but a trot just the same. Papa threw his head back and laughed.

"Bud!" yelled Rachel. She waved her arms furiously. "Over here! Bud!" She jumped from Papa's saddle into Papa's arms, and he lowered her quickly but gently to the ground. Off she ran behind her mother. This was no time to be a lady.

Between Mama's hugs and Rachel's neck holds, they nearly squeezed the very breath out of Bud. Then Mama stepped back and exclaimed,

"Oh, my Bud! Just look at you!"

There he stood in a soldier's uniform, looking taller than Rachel had remembered and definitely much thinner. He wore gray wool pants and the dark blue frock coat that he had worn at military school. Rachel had always liked that coat because of the two rows of gold buttons that ran down each side of Bud's chest, making him look like a real general. Because the Confederacy had not yet issued regulatory uniforms to the new army, each soldier had to do the best he could with regard to dress. Rachel noticed that other soldiers had on similar coats as Bud;

probably they too had gone to a military academy. But others had on simple wool or flannel pants and shirts, varying in color from butternut brown to dark blue.

Draped over Bud's shoulder was a leather strap that ended with a saber that hung clumsily from his hip. He had a small pistol attached to his belt on the other side. When Mama asked Bud about the saber, he confessed that he had borrowed it from a prominent citizen in town just for the occasion and had to return it tomorrow. Rachel thought Bud looked weighted down and asked,

"Can you march with all that stuff hangin' off you?"

"Sure can, Little Bit," he grinned, using a pet name he had started calling Rachel when he'd gone to military school. "In fact, this is nothin' compared to what we'll have to carry on a real march."

And then he began to describe and demonstrate how a second shoulder strap would carry a cartridge box alongside his pistol, another strap for a canteen, and a third for a haversack that contained rations and personal things. If the troops were moving to a new camp, there was usually a bed roll loaded on their back, plus the tall rifles that had to be toted. All this could have sounded like complaining on Bud's part if he hadn't shown so much pride in it all. Mama and Rachel reacted by being duly impressed.

"Where's your horse?" Rachel was looking around. "Where's Lightning?"

"He's in the camp corral..." Bud started to explain, but just then, Suzanna Wade burst upon them, and Bud's attention was swept away. Where did she come from,

Rachel wanted to know. Rachel stuck out her bottom lip and scowled. She didn't like sharing her brother with a silly girl. Surely Bud wouldn't waste his time talking to her. Rachel was sure if he'd just ignore Suzanna, she'd soon go away. But, to Rachel's dismay, Bud seemed to be extremely pleased to see her.

Mama and Papa steered Rachel away from Bud so he could have a few moments alone with Suzanna. Papa continued to explain about Lightning.

"You see, hon'," Papa was saying. "Bud's chosen to be in the infantry. That means, he's a foot soldier. They don't ride horses, but he's keeping Lightning here to use when he needs him."

Papa looked at Mama and added, "Bud's been made a second lieutenant in his company because of his time at the military academy. That's why he chose to stay in infantry."

Papa knelt down to see eye-to-eye with Rachel.

"Your papa's in the cavalry," he grinned. "That's why I get to ride my horse all the time."

"Are you a second lieutenant, Papa?" asked Rachel.

"No," he answered and looked at Mama again. "I'm a major."

Then Papa pulled out his pocket watch and looked at the time.

"And this major must get his men together," Papa lifted Rachel up onto the horse again. He turned and wrapped his arm around Mama's waist. "So, ladies, let's be off to the grandstand."

They all turned to call goodbye to Bud who was holding both of Suzanna Wade's white-gloved hands in his own. His face was an odd color of red, and he had a silly grin on his face that Rachel had never seen before. Rachel studied Suzanna Wade for a few seconds. She was tall and slender with brown hair that was pinned back under a small blue hat. Soft, long ringlets hung down her back, and her eyes were a dark brown. Rachel supposed she was pretty enough but not so deserving of all the attention Bud was giving her. As Papa led the horse away Rachel caught a glimpse of a short but tender kiss between the two. She covered her mouth and giggled.

"What about Laura?" Mama seemed to have forgotten her young friend until just now. She turned and searched the crowd for her, but Evan and Miss Laura were nowhere to be seen.

"I'm sure Miss Laura is in good hands," Papa smiled and squeezed Mama's waist. "They're probably headed for the grandstand now."

The parade of soldiers was more spectacular than Rachel could ever have imagined. Rows and rows of stiff, straight-shouldered soldiers passed by as everyone cheered and waved flags or handkerchiefs. All the drilling, drilling, drilling Bud had complained about in his letters certainly paid off, for each company stepped precisely together, keeping their lines straight as they passed by. Sun glints sparkled off the shiny silver bayonets of hundreds of rifles, making Rachel cover her eyes with a paper fan someone had given her.

Rachel and Mama watched anxiously for Papa and Bud to march by, and when they first caught sight of Bud, they both stood up, waving to him frantically with their handkerchiefs. Although it was impossible to be heard above the cheering crowd, Rachel called to Bud in her loudest, unlady-like voice. It was hard to tell if Bud saw or heard them because, being a good second lieutenant, he kept his eyes straight ahead. Rachel smiled when she saw her blue ribbon tied to a button on his jacket. It pleased her to think he had not lost it in all this time. But her smile disappeared when she noticed there was a second ribbon, a yellow one, tied to his jacket as well. She didn't have to guess who had given Bud that one, and the sight of it made Rachel scowl again.

The rest of the day was filled with speeches and cheering, and more speeches and more cheering. Politicians stood at the podium with their chests puffed out, either from pride or 'hot air' or both, and gave eloquent speeches. Patriotism flowed like water, and hearts beat fiercely with Confederate pride. The band played "Dixie" and other down-home melodies to stir the spirit and bring people to their feet. Everyone seemed to be filled with an overwhelming sense of victory even though a single shot of the war had yet to be fired.

Rachel soon tired of big words and endless applauding, and she began to fidget. She wished she were sitting with Papa atop his horse, and they could ride away from all the noise and people. Her mind was completely absorbed in this wonderful daydream when she was jolted back to reality by hearing the name Suzanna Wade. Rachel sat up and looked toward the speaker's stand.

There stood Suzanna holding the flag she and Mama and the other ladies had worked so diligently on, the very flag upon which she had shed blood and because of which had suffered sore fingers. The prettiest young belles had been chosen to present flags to the troops, and Suzanna was blushing as she now spoke about the honor that had been bestowed upon her. She said a few words that echoed everybody else who had spoken already, how we love our dear brave soldiers, how our hearts go into battle with them, and so on and so forth.

Rachel let out a big snort and crossed her arms in front of her. She was angry that Suzanna had been chosen to present her flag. It should've been someone else to do the honors, anyone else, even mousey, freckled-faced GeorgeAnne Grimes would have suited Rachel just fine. She puffed up like a big, fat bullfrog and stuck her bottom lip out in a pout. It was a good thing no one was paying any attention to her, or else she would have been scolded severely.

Having finished saying her few words, Suzanna Wade handed the folded flag to Bud's commanding officer and then, in front of everybody, gave the man a peck on the cheek.

"Well," Rachel thought to herself in a huff. "I hope Bud saw that. He might think twice about wearing that yellow ribbon."

What she later learned was that each chosen belle did

precisely the same thing as Suzanna did—made a short speech, presented the flag, and gave a lucky officer a kiss on the cheek. It didn't matter to Rachel, though, and she would've stewed about it all day had it not been for all the busy activities going on.

The two days they stayed in Jackson were like a whirlwind and ended much too quickly for Rachel and Mama. Before they knew it, they were waving goodbye to Papa and Bud. Papa was headed north into Tennessee, and Bud was marching south toward New Orleans. There was no telling when they might see either of them next, and it made the farewells even more painful than the first time they had left for war.

The three travelers were once again seated on the old buckboard wagon, now empty of all its supplies and rattling noisily as they bounced along. Rachel studied Mama's face and could see that all the excitement had drained from it, replaced by a very solemn, worried look. The feelings of uncertainty and dread hung heavily in the air as their home came into view. Rachel wondered if Mama and she could manage alone. It would be hard, very hard, and Rachel was not sure if she were brave enough to do it.

As she drifted to sleep in her own bed again, Rachel's heart ached. It ached from wishing so hard that all of this war would just go away. She wanted it to be a bad dream from which she would wake up. And she fell asleep with tears on her pillow, knowing it was not a dream.

5

In the Midst of the Storm

august, 1861

THE NEWS SPREAD QUICKLY. From northern Virginia to the
borders of Texas to the tip of Florida, the Confederate
States of America throbbed as one heart with the pulse
of victory. It was the first real battle of the Civil War, and
it had been won by the Confederacy. No true-blooded
Southerner was surprised. They had not expected otherwise.

It had happened on a Sunday, the twenty-first of
July, in Virginia at a place called Manassas Junction
on Bull Run Creek. It was an important railroad junction that led west directly into Manassas Gap through
the Shenandoah Valley. Whoever controlled that gap

could shift troops quickly from one side of the Blue Ridge Mountains to the other. Controlling Manassas Junction also meant controlling northern Virginia and, eventually, the Confederate capital, Richmond. Had the Union succeeded in seizing Manassas Junction and Gap, it would have been a swift end to the 'rebellion.'

People buzzed about the battle for days on end, and Rachel loved to hear the stories that went along with it. She especially liked to hear how Congressmen, important businessmen, and ladies carrying parasols and picnic baskets had come out in their buggies from Washington to have a holiday and watch the Yankees crush the Rebel army, only to be nearly run over by the retreating Union soldiers who made it back across the Potomac River before them. It was even rumored that a Congressman had been found hiding behind a tree during the battle and had been taken as a prisoner to Richmond. It was a story that brought loud roars of laughter each time it was repeated.

New southern heroes had emerged overnight, giving even more hope to the southern people. General P.G.T. Beauregard, the Creole hero of Fort Sumter, was once more wrapped in glory as the officer behind the Union rout, although General Joe Johnston, a distinguished veteran of the Old Army, was actually the commanding general. Rachel's favorite of all was the story of T.J. Jackson, a Virginia general, who lined his men on the crest of a hill and stood like a stone wall until the Yankees came almost face-to-face with his men; then he sent the Yanks

tumbling back down the hill in a wall of gunfire. People everywhere were calling the professor-turned-hero 'Stonewall' Jackson, a name that would forever stick.

Although Mama and Rachel were relieved that neither Papa nor Bud were involved in the battle, they were saddened by the ever-growing list of casualties. It was reported that at least 387 Rebel soldiers had been killed and around 1,500 wounded, including sons of the cotton states — Mississippi, Alabama, and Georgia. Mama shivered each time she read these reports, no doubt thinking of all the grief-stricken mothers, wives, and children.

Blood had indeed been shed for independence, enough blood, it would seem. The war was surely over now; at least that was what everyone was saying. Miss Rosalee Prentiss had said so herself as she and her doctor husband had dined on the following Sunday with Mama and Rachel.

"Well, of course, the war's over, dears," she had proclaimed. "It's very plain to see the Yankees can't whip our boys, or even put up a good fight. Your men'll be coming home soon enough, you mark my words."

And with that said, she had stuffed her mouth with a strawberry cream puff while Dr. Prentiss, his mouth already stuffed, had nodded his head in agreement. Rachel's heart had pounded with the thought of Papa and Bud coming home, and the first chance she got, she ran to tell Lizbet.

"Papa's comin' home!" she had exclaimed, completely out of breath from running across the yard to the clothesline where Lizbet was hanging out the clothes.

"Missuh William comin' home?" Lizbet had echoed in surprise. "When? Today?"

"No, not today," Rachel answered. "At least I don't think today. But the war's over, and they're comin' home."

"Da war's already o-vuh?" Lizbet scratched her braided head. "Who won?"

"Well, we did, of course," Rachel laughed out loud. "Bud said it'd be over at the end of the summer, and he was right."

Rachel laughed again out of sheer happiness. Then she stopped and stared at her friend's expression.

"Aren't you happy?" she asked Lizbet. "We won. We beat the Yankees."

Lizbet nodded her head slowly. Her eyes were staring at a wet pillowcase in her hands. She seemed to be thinking really hard.

"Dis mean dey be no freedom?" she asked innocently.

"Freedom?" Rachel was surprised. "What do you mean? We have freedom. We're free from the Yankees, for sure. An' that means we're free to do exactly what we want to do."

Lizbet nodded in agreement, but slowly, and her expression did not change. She was still thinking hard.

"I means freedom fo' *us*," she explained. "You know... what da Yankees promise. To free all us."

Rachel was confused. "Why do you need freedom, Lizbet? This is your home, *our* home. We have everything we need here. Doesn't Papa look after you? Aren't you happy here? What would you do… where would you go… if you had freedom?"

"Don't know," Lizbet shrugged her shoulders and looked down at the pillowcase, still dripping in her hands. She stretched up her arms, put the piece of cloth next to the line, and jammed a wooden peg down on it. "No, suh, I don't knows what I do. But I be free to do it. Dat's all."

Lizbet looked over at her friend and smiled, showing all her white teeth. But Rachel didn't smile back. She was still confused, and hurt, to think Lizbet would want to leave their home. She felt her face start to quiver and was afraid she might burst out crying, so she turned away quickly and headed for the house. She didn't want to think about what Lizbet had just said. Her eyes stung with tears that she couldn't fight back. She would go to her room and think only of Papa and Bud coming home and everything being the way it was before.

Day after day Rachel waited for Papa or Bud to come home. She watched the long road that led to their house for dust clouds that signaled a rider approaching. But all was still and quiet. The days were scorching hot and heavy with humidity. It was already the middle of August, and neither of them had come home. Nothing had happened. Until one afternoon a messenger brought a letter from Papa with the bad news.

The war had not ended with the Battle of Bull Run, as it was being called. Even though the Yankees had lost more men in the fight, 460 killed, over 1,000 wounded, and an astounding 1,300 taken as prisoners, they were not giving up. President Lincoln would not agree to let the Confederacy have their own government and would *never* agree to it.

Mama sighed as she read the numbers.

"Enough blood has *not* been shed, I guess," she whispered to herself.

She continued to read the letter aloud. Papa was still in Tennessee but planning to move camp soon. Mama's face softened and almost lit up as Papa mentioned he would try to make a quick trip home to check on the cotton crop and, of course, his two darlings. Rachel clapped her hands and squealed with delight. It would be better than Christmas morning to have her father gallop up to the front porch, even if it were only for a day.

Suddenly, there was pounding at the front door. Mama dropped Papa's letter on the floor, lifted her heavy skirts, and hurried to the window. She pulled back the sheer lace curtain and peeked out.

"It's Mr. Johnson," she whispered, "from down by the mill."

In one swift movement Mama turned and headed toward the door as she gripped Rachel's arm to keep her in place.

"You stay here, sweetheart," Mama insisted. She let go of Rachel and disappeared from the parlor.

Obeying her mother Rachel stayed in her spot, but she strained to hear what the voices were saying. Mr. Johnson sounded as though he was in a state of panic. His voice

was high and nervous, but all Rachel could understand were his pleas of 'Hurry' and 'Please, ma'am.'

Rachel heard the door slam at the same instant Mama called out for Lily. It was very unusual for Mama to yell for anyone, especially inside the house, and Rachel knew something was wrong. She ran after her mother who was already at the kitchen door.

"What's wrong, Mama?" Rachel called. But Mama had disappeared behind the kitchen door and did not answer her. When Rachel reached the kitchen, Mama was busy giving orders to everyone.

"Lizbet," Mama was saying, "go tell Josup to bring the carriage around to the front. Go quickly, child. Tell him to hurry. There's not much time."

Then Mama turned her attention to Lily.

"Gather a stack of linens, Lily, and come with me," Mama turned to go, then stopped and added, "And find a basket, a big one, and bring it, too."

Mama whirled around again, almost running over her daughter who was still waiting for an answer and was becoming somewhat distressed.

"Oh, there you are," Mama knelt down to Rachel's eye level, took her by the shoulders, and said, "Now, hon', I'll be gone for a while. I'm taking Josup and Lily with me. You stay here with Lizbet. You'll be all right till I get home."

"But, Mama," Rachel was really distressed now. "What's wrong? What's happened?"

"Mae Johnson's having her baby," Mama straightened up and headed for the door. "She needs help. Dr. Prentiss is in the next county and can't make it in time. I've got to go."

Then, like a whirlwind, Mama, Lily, and Josup loaded the carriage and took off in a cloud of dust. Rachel and Lizbet watched the dust cloud as far as they could see it. Both girls gave a sigh and sat down on the front steps. They felt as if a storm had just passed through, leaving them in a strange stillness. Rachel shivered, certainly not from being cold, for it was another stifling, hot day, but from an eerie feeling that came over her whole body. A feeling that something bad was going to happen. And she was right. The storm had not yet come, and she would soon be more frightened than she had ever been in her life.

Rachel and Lizbet sat with heads together on the back porch. With the adults gone, they would have lots of glorious, uninterrupted time to read one of Rachel's books. It was a rare treat. There had not been much time lately for Lizbet to practice her reading, and she was struggling especially hard now.

"Dis too hawd," Lizbet complained. "My head be hurtin'."

Rachel scowled with skepticism. "Readin' doesn't make your head hurt." She played the part of the stern school mistress. "Keep readin'."

"It do make my head hurt," Lizbet insisted. She rubbed her forehead to prove it.

Rachel relented with a sigh and put the book in her own lap. She began reading aloud, and Lizbet grinned broadly. Rachel cut her eyes at her friend whose head didn't seem to hurt so much now but continued to read. They both became so absorbed in the story that neither of them realized how much time had passed, that the afternoon sun had dropped low in the sky, and it was getting late. Neither of them saw the huge black cloud that rolled across the sky, blocking out the light, until Rachel could no longer see the words on the page.

Both girls now stared up at the ominous sky. They watched as the blackness grew thicker and tumbled over the remaining blue sky. They heard the low, faraway rumble of thunder, and they looked at each other for reassurance.

Suddenly, the wind began to blow hard, flipping the book off Rachel's lap in one big gust. The girls jumped up together, whisked up the book, and in two leaps, they were across the back porch and inside the door. Breathlessly they leaned against the closed door as if to keep out the storm and panted like two foxes begin chased by hounds.

The house was dark. As the windows rattled and the walls creaked from the strong winds, Rachel and Lizbet realized they were all alone, and it wasn't at all glorious now. They wished for their mothers. Their mothers would light a lamp or candle and tell them everything would be just fine. It was pitch black now, and the girls knew they needed to light a lamp. But they were frozen against the door as the wind howled louder.

A sudden clap of thunder jolted Rachel and Lizbet out of their state of paralysis. Lizbet knew where to find a lamp, even in the dark. She groped across the room with one hand and held onto Rachel with the other. They managed to light a large oil lamp just as the rains came. In loud swooshing sound it beat against the windows.

Rachel and Lizbet sat down at the table with the oil lamp between them. Shadows danced in the flicker of the small flame. Sudden flashes of lightning gave life to the things in the room. Both girls stared at each other with wide eyes, afraid to move or speak.

Then somehow, between the loud crashes of thunder and the roar of wind and rain, they heard a noise on the porch. Footsteps.

They waited. There it was again. Yes, it was footsteps stomping across the porch.

Both girls shouted, "Mama!" and spun around, hoping to see their mothers come rushing, soaking wet, in the backdoor.

But, it was not their mothers. Rachel and Lizbet gasped at the same time. The black outline of the figure that they saw moving past the windows was big and bulky, not at all like Mama or Lily or even Josup.

They waited again and strained to hear where the footsteps were going. Maybe the stranger was just getting out of the storm. Maybe he was simply waiting on the porch until the storm passed.

Both girls held their breaths. Afraid to move a muscle or blink an eye, they watched the figure move past the

window closest to the backdoor. Both sets of eyes locked on the window on the other side of the door, hoping to see the shadow go past there as well.

But it didn't. And in the next instant there was pounding on the door.

Loud, insistent pounding that echoed the terribly loud thunder that sounded every few minutes. The shadowy faces of the two girls stared at each other in silent terror. Lizbet reached across the table and squeezed Rachel's hands so hard she almost cried out.

Rachel was frozen with fear. She was thinking to shake her head 'no' to signal Lizbet to stay put, but she wasn't sure if her head was moving at all. She wanted to put out the lamp but couldn't let go of Lizbet's hands to reach it.

"Mitz' Franklin!" a voice called out. "Open za door!"

At the same time Rachel and Lizbet sucked in big gasps of air. It was Mr. Gunther. Right here on their porch, trying to get in their house. What was he doing here? What could he want?

Rachel didn't know what to do. She tried to think what Mama would do if she were here. Mama would be brave. She would march right over to the door, open it, and let Mr. Gunther come out of the storm. But Rachel was too afraid.

"Please, Mitz'! It's Goonter," the voice shouted again. But this time, it sounded pleading and urgent, like Mr. Johnson's had sounded earlier today.

Something was wrong. Rachel was sure of it. Somebody might be hurt or sick, or worse yet, having a baby. Rachel moved to get up. Terrified Lizbet tightened her grip on Rachel's hands, digging her fingernails into Rachel's skin, and shook her head furiously.

"Let go. I've got to see what he wants," Rachel whispered through clenched teeth as she peeled Lizbet's fingers off her hands.

"No!" Lizbet whispered back excitedly. "He a bad man. He gone kill you."

Rachel gulped. She thought of Mr. Gunther's scary eye and his rough, red face. She wasn't sure what he would do. But she knew she had to find out.

With trembling hands Rachel grabbed the doorknob. She glanced back across the dark room for a reassuring look from Lizbet, but her friend was nowhere to be seen. Probably hiding in the dark shadows or under the table. Rachel took a big breath and pulled the door open.

Mr. Gunther's large boot was inside the door in the next instant. His strong arm pushed the door right out of Rachel's hand, and it flew back with the heavy wind and rain. Rachel was drenched in a split second.

And just as quickly, Mr. Gunther pulled the door back and shut it behind him. He grabbed both Rachel's arms with his strong hands almost picking her off the floor. Rachel held her breath and prayed it wasn't the end.

"Where ist your mut-ter?" Mr. Gunther said loudly, still trying to be heard over the raging storm.

"She's gone," replied Rachel in a similarly loud voice. "But she'll be back any minute now."

Rachel looked around the room again, but still no sign of Lizbet. Rachel tried not to look at Mr. Gunther's bad eye, but right now the good one was staring at her desperately. He was totally distraught, and Rachel was afraid he might cry.

Just then the wind died down, and the rain stopped beating against the house. The lightning was not so intense as before, and the thunder seemed to be moving farther and farther away. Outside the storm was passing, but the one inside the house was still going strong. Mr. Gunther continued to hold Rachel by the arms, and in his excitement, he was shaking her as he spoke.

"I nee't her to come quickly," Mr. Gunther began to explain. "My boy, my Henrich, has run off to za war. And my Eltza is a mad woman."

Mr. Gunther finally let go of Rachel and walked to the window. He paced to the next window as if his movement would make Mama's carriage appear. Rachel's heart was beating frantically, and it was hard to breathe. She did not know what to do with this man gone mad himself. If only Mama would get home right now.

If the storm had been loud and frightening before, the calm and quiet was even more frightening now. The rain had stopped altogether, and only the drips from the eaves and trees could be heard. Rachel kept her eyes glued to Mr. Gunther, watching him pace. Finally, he stopped at

one of the windows, put his fists on the windowsill, and rested his forehead on the pane. He didn't look so scary anymore, Rachel thought, just sad and tired.

Then, Rachel's prayers were answered. The sound of a carriage could be heard coming close to the back of the house.

"Mama!" Rachel yelled in her excitement. She leaped to the door, flung it open, and ran across the porch.

Josup was pulling up the reins to stop the horse and the carriage right by the porch steps. Mama and Lily crawled out slowly, looking very tired.

"Mama!" Rachel bolted down the steps, nearly knocking Mama backward as she bear-hugged her around the waist.

"Oh, hon', I'm so sorry we're late," Mama apologized, wrapping her arms around her daughter. "We got caught in the storm and had to wait it out in Swaggart's barn. I thought it'd never pass."

Mama pulled Rachel back so she could see her face.

"Are you all right?" she asked. "And what about Lizbet? Is she all right?"

Mama looked around. "Where is she anyway?"

"Hidin' in the house somewhere," Rachel said and ignored the funny look on Mama's face. "Mama… Mr. Gunther's in the kitchen … and he's awful upset."

Mama's face changed from motherly concern to deep worry. She walked past Rachel, up the steps, and was across the porch in two giant steps. Mr. Gunther was standing at the door waiting for her.

"Mitz' Franklin," he began calmly now that she was home. "Itz my Eltza. She's in an awful state. Loo-zing her mind, I t'ink."

Mama was studying Mr. Gunther's face intently so she could understand what he was saying.

"What's happened to her?" Mama asked.

"My boy, my Henrich, has run off to za war," Mr. Gunther was running his hands through his hair nervously. "I don't know what got into him. But he's gone. And... and my Eltza... she's gone mad."

He looked straight into Mama's face.

"And I don't know what to do," Mr. Gunther looked as if he were about to bawl. "I t'ought you might talk witz her. Seeing as you have two men in za war."

Although exhaustion was written all over Mama's face, she quickly answered,

"Of course, of course."

Then she turned to Josup who was just unhitching the horse from its harness.

"Put it back on, Josup," Mama instructed. "Take me down to the Gunthers and quickly."

Old, tired Josup didn't change expression but simply began rehitching the equally tired horse. Mama motioned for Mr. Gunther to get in the carriage, but he declined. He knew it would not be proper for him to ride with Mrs.

Franklin in her carriage. He would take a short-cut and promised to be there at about the same time.

So, Mama was off again. Lily stayed this time, so at least Lizbet could come out of hiding. Rachel called out as the carriage started away.

"What was it?"

Mama peeked over the side of the carriage.

"What was what?" she called back.

"The baby," Rachel raised her voice to be heard.

"A boy!" Mama yelled as the carriage disappeared behind the barn. "It was a boy!"

6

An Unexpected Visit

september, 1861

BY THE END OF SEPTEMBER the fields were bulging with fluffy, white cotton. If the fields could talk they would be screaming to be picked. But whether or not that would happen was another matter. With Mr. Gunther having gone just about as mad as his wife and spending most of his time wandering around the country looking for his son, there was no one to organize the pickers and get the job started.

"Dat Gunt'er man done gone mad hisself," Lily had grumbled as she watched Mama hurrying out to check on the fields. "Po' Missus has all dis worry."

Poor Mama was right! All the burdens of managing a plantation rested on her shoulders, and it was beginning to show. Her face was always strained with worry. There were dark circles under her eyes from loss of sleep. Not only did problems arise every day but during the night as well, and it was not unusual for Mama to be awakened from her sleep by pounding on the door. There seemed to be no end of things to be done. And no sign of Papa.

Right now Mama was overseeing the butchering of a hog. Rachel thought it was a ghastly sight to see the dead hog hung upside-down by his hind feet and slit open right down the middle. She shuddered just thinking about it. Mama had scolded her for making such a fuss about it.

"Come this winter you'll be glad for that butchering," Mama had said, "when you've got delicious ham for breakfast."

Before Mama left she instructed Rachel to read her history lesson, then write in her journal, and after that, practice her scales on the piano. Rachel made an ugly, scowling face but not where Mama could see. She hated to be doing such silly things when a war was going on. She could certainly understand why Gunther's boy, Henry, had run off to the war. It was much more noble to fight for one's country than sit at home and read about it.

Rachel lay on the sofa in the parlor with her head propped on the history book. She listened to the silence and daydreamed. She dreamed about being in a camp with rows and rows of white tents and campfires to sit by at night. She remembered all the young soldiers in the parade back in July, and the pride that showed on their faces. She wished she could wear a uniform with shiny gold buttons like Bud or ride on a spirited horse like Papa. How exciting that would be!

Rachel was so deep in daydreaming about the war that she didn't hear the horse approaching. She didn't hear the boots stomping across the front porch. She only heard the door open, and she shot up off the sofa in one leap. A man in dark gray pants and a long gray coat came into the hall and, with his back to Rachel, looked into the dining room. Rachel held her breath and did not move.

In a split second the man turned to face the parlor where Rachel stood, and she let out the loudest scream ever.

"Papa! Papa!" she cried and ran to him. Papa swooped her up in his arms and squeezed her really hard. He didn't say a word but buried his head in her soft curls as if getting his very breath from the smell of her hair.

After a few minutes he let her down and asked, "Where's your mother?"

"She's gone to kill a hog," Rachel replied.

"She's what?" Papa couldn't hide his surprise.

"She's gone to…"

Papa interrupted Rachel. "I know what you said, dear. But your mother… butchering hogs?"

He knelt to Rachel's eye level and added, "That's Gunther's job." Papa's face turned grim. "Where's Mr. Gunther?"

Rachel sighed. "Well, Papa, it's a long story. Henry ran off to the war and Mis' Gunther lost her mind and

Mr. Gunther came in a terrible storm and banged on the door and…"

Papa had heard enough. He was down the hall, through the kitchen, and out the back door before Rachel could finish her tale and catch her breath. She turned and ran after him.

"Papa, wait! Wait for me!" she called.

But Papa stopped at the back door and shook his head.

"I need you to stay here and do a job for me," he said. "Go find Lily and tell her I'm home. Tell her I'd like a berry pie. I'll be back soon... with your mother."

That night at dinner Mama and Rachel listened intently to every word Papa said. He talked about the troops, the bad food, the mosquitoes, the patrols, just about everything he had done in the last few months. Papa was sorry he didn't have news about Bud, but Mama said it was all right because she did. Bud's letters had continued to arrive although not nearly as often as in early summer. The last she had heard from Bud he was still camped near the Gulf Coast, close at hand for the defenses of New Orleans or Mobile. Papa nodded his head thoughtfully and reached over for the ten-thousandth time and patted Mama's hand.

Throughout their meal Papa had patted the hands of his two 'darlings,' first Mama's delicate small hand, then Rachel's even smaller one. He couldn't seem to eat for wanting to touch them. And it was the same for Mama and Rachel. They couldn't take their eyes off Papa but stared at him lovingly as he talked. Rachel liked his more rugged face, the dark tan from so many hours in the saddle, the moustache, and, of course, his dark blue eyes that seemed even darker and bluer.

When Papa had finished his second helping of Lily's berry pie the three of them moved into the parlor to stretch out. Rachel curled up beside Papa on the sofa, putting her head in his lap. Mama pulled her chair closer to the sofa so she could hold Papa's hand. They sat for a long time enjoying the sound of crickets and a soft night breeze.

Then Papa began to talk about the war again. But this time he spoke about changes and plans and all sorts of serious things Rachel didn't understand. It was soothing just to hear the sound of his voice, and she was content to listen as he stroked her hair and talked to Mama.

"The Union's got a strange idea on how to win the war. People are calling it the Anaconda Plan," Papa chuckled softly. "It's really a joke, if you ask me, but in theory, it sounds like a reasonable plan."

Half asleep Rachel heard the funny word.

"What's anaconda, Papa?"

Papa looked down at Rachel, thinking she had been asleep.

"An anaconda is actually an animal," he explained, "a huge snake."

"Is Bud gonna have to fight snakes?" she asked. "He's good at fightin' snakes."

Papa and Mama both laughed out loud. Rachel didn't know what was so funny, but it was good to hear them both laugh, and it made her laugh, too.

"No, dear, no," Papa stopped laughing and continued to explain. "Anaconda is just a name the Union has used. It describes the way in which they want to cut the Confederacy off from the rest of the world."

Papa shifted his position on the sofa to get more comfortable, making Rachel's head rock.

"You see, an anaconda doesn't kill its prey by a poison-

ous bite like our cotton-mouths do. It wraps its long body around and around the prey and then squeezes the very life out of it."

Rachel shivered. She hated snakes and thinking about them gave her the willies.

"So what do snakes have to do with the war, Papa?"

"Nothing, nothing at all," Papa sighed. He realized things had gotten way off the subject, and he was trying to find a way to get back on track. "The Union has the idea that it can surround the Confederacy, take the Mississippi River, all the coastal ports and border states on the north, and squeeze the life out of us just like the anaconda."

Rachel thought about this for a while. She closed her eyes as if to drift off to sleep and said,

"I hope we don't get squeezed that hard 'cause I think it would really hurt."

Papa continued to talk to Mama about the 'squeeze' on the South. Prices on necessary goods, like salt, sugar, coffee, were already going up, but Papa predicted things would get worse, much worse. He instructed her on how to conserve their bought goods and what to store up for the winter. Then his voice dropped to almost a whisper. Rachel could barely hear what he was saying.

"Belle, you need to hide all the silver, jewelry, any valuables," he instructed. "Do it yourself, and don't let anyone know where you've put it."

It was a good thing Mama wasn't the kind of woman to fret and get all upset or she'd be swooning from the mere thought of all this. It was really scary to Rachel, and

she didn't like hearing Papa talk about how bad things might be. Surely no Yankees would ever come on their land or near their house. It was unthinkable.

Papa explained to Mama about the new Confederate money. Of course, it was only good in the South which made exchanging one's wealth for the new bills a risky business, Papa thought. In order to support the Confederacy Papa was obligated to exchange his money for the new bills and yes, he would. But he was cautious enough to keep a large portion of their assets in gold and silver.

There was a long silence. Rachel thought her parents may have fallen to sleep. She opened her eye, tilted her head slightly, and saw that her father and mother were deep in thought. Papa was trying to remember everything he had needed to tell Mama, and Mama was trying to absorb all that she had been told.

Finally, Mama broke the silence.

"Will there be more fighting, William?" she asked.

Papa looked at her with sad, serious eyes. He sighed and nodded his head.

"I'm afraid so," he answered. "President Lincoln has appointed a new general of his Army of the Potomac, George B. McClellan, a real 'Napoleon' the papers say. The North's answer to our dashing Beauregard, I read in one account."

Papa snorted in disgust. "He's the pride of the Union, this 'Little Mac.'"

Papa noticed Mama's funny look on hearing that nickname. "That's what his soldiers call him... in a most

endearing way, I assure you."

Papa sighed again. "He's building up quite an army, I hear. I'm sure the next battle in Virginia won't be as bungled as Bull Run. One thing is for certain... our boys'll be outnumbered. Hopefully, not out-fought."

This was too much even for a strong woman like Mama. She was upset now and looked as if she might cry. Papa lifted her hand to his lips. They had talked enough about war and hard times and the unknown future.

"There, there," Papa tried to soothe his wife. He kissed her hand again. "It might not come to anything at all. Each day brings something new, and all of this might be over by Christmas."

It was getting late, and they both decided it was time for bed. Papa lifted Rachel up onto his lap and stood up, holding her like a rag doll. Sometime between the talk of gold and Little Mac Rachel had fallen asleep. Papa took her upstairs to her bedroom. As he laid her on the bed Rachel muttered,

"Papa, will you be here in the morning?"

"Yes, dear," he whispered. "I'll be here, I promise."

Rachel smiled as she drifted back to sleep. Papa leaned to give Rachel a good-night kiss on the forehead.

"Papa, will you stay home for good now?"

"I wish I could," he sighed. "But I have to go back in a few days."

"How many days?" Rachel wanted to know before she fell asleep for good.

"Three days," Papa replied. "I can stay for three days."

"Promise?" she insisted.

"Yes, dear, I promise."

But it was a promise Papa could not keep.

The next morning the small family sat down together for a delicious breakfast. It was a beautiful fall day, still warm as it always is in September in the South. Papa had been up before the sun to make sure the pickers were in the fields. Mama was relieved to have him here to take over, and everyone was in a cheerful mood. Lily's biscuits never tasted so good, Rachel thought.

But their peaceful moment was suddenly interrupted by the sound of horses' hooves. A rider was galloping right up to their front porch. Papa jumped up from his chair. Mama and Rachel both held their breaths as he opened the door. They listened to a few muttered words, and then the door closed again. Papa stepped back into the dining room with a small piece of paper in his hand. Mama's face went pale. Her first thought was always of Bud.

"It's a message from my commander," Papa announced sadly.

Mama let out a sigh, but the worried look on her face did not disappear, only worsened. Rachel felt tears come to her eyes.

Papa saw the looks of dismay and could hardly get the words out.

"I've been ordered back to camp," his voice was weak and shaky. "I've got to leave right away."

Mama ran to her husband, clutching him and burying her face in his chest. "Oh, William, oh William" was all she could say.

Rachel lowered her head and sobbed. She couldn't bear to see her father leave so soon. He had only just gotten here, and it wasn't fair that he should have to go now.

Still clutching Mama, Papa moved to Rachel and lifted her from the chair. He held her tightly, breathing in the smell of her hair as he had done when he first arrived just the day before. He wanted to remember that smell and the soft touch of her cheek. He wiped away his daughter's tears and studied her eyes to remember the pretty blue of them. While holding Rachel with one arm and the other arm wrapped around Mama, he pulled the two tightly to him. The three clung together in silence. Papa was savoring this moment with his wife and child to keep in his memory for the long days ahead.

And like a good dream that is over too soon, Papa was gone away.

7

Walking into a Nightmare

october, 1861

NORMALLY, MAMA AND RACHEL would've moped for days after Papa's sudden and disappointing departure. But there was simply too much to do to dwell on it. Besides, thoughts of Papa and Bud, battles and war, were almost too painful and frightening. It was a blessing in disguise to be too busy for thinking. Even Rachel's school work was put on hold as she was required to help her mother with simple tasks. Rachel was even getting used to being awakened before the sun was up to get instructions from Mama before she headed to the fields.

"Wake up, Rachel," Mama said in a soft but firm voice. "Wake up, dear."

Rachel sat up and rubbed her eyes. The room was still dark, and she could barely make out her mother's face in the flicker of her candle.

"Are you awake, dear?" Mama asked.

"Yes, Mama," answered Rachel, although she wasn't sure how awake she was.

"Listen to me, sweetheart," Mama sat on the edge of the bed and brushed Rachel's hair with her fingers as she gave the day's instructions. "After breakfast I need you to go to the Gunther's place and check on Mrs. Gunther. Can you do that for me?"

"Yes, ma'am," Rachel said obediently, but she wasn't at all sure if she was hearing her mother correctly. Surely Mama didn't expect her to go all the way to the Gunther's, who lived near the bayou where it was swampy and snaky, all by herself.

"Take her a loaf of bread Lily's baked this morning," she added, "and a crock of butter... and some buttermilk. Can you remember all that?"

"Yes, ma'am," Rachel gave a big yawn and thought hard about what Mama was telling her.

"I'm afraid Mrs. Gunther's not doing well," Mama stood up, ready to be on her way. "We need to keep a close eye on her... Mr. Gunther being gone and all. She doesn't need to be alone."

Mama moved toward the door, taking the candle and leaving Rachel in the dark again.

"Sleep a little longer, dear," Mama's voice sounded soft and caring. "But don't forget what I've told you to do."

Rachel did go back to sleep, but not for long. As soon as the first rays of the sun peeped through her window she was up. She washed her face, neck, and hands in a large bowl on her vanity that had been filled with water by either Jo or Mott while she was still sleeping. She fumbled nervously with the buttons on her blouse. Going to the Gunthers was not a walk she was eager to make.

Rachel ate breakfast in the kitchen with Lily and Lizbet. This morning Lily had made hot cakes with molasses, grits, and pork meat. The three of them ate in silence until Rachel finally spoke up.

"Mama's sendin' me to see about Mrs. Gunther."

Lizbet's eyes got big with surprise.

"You gone to dat house?" she asked in disbelief. "Dat woman be cra-a-a-zy. An' dere be snakes!"

"Hush, chile," Lily scolded. "She down wit' da madness 'cause she done lost three sons, dat's all."

Lizbet looked down at her plate in shame, but her big brown eyes popped back up to look at Rachel. The whites of her eyes were large, and there was a look of 'better-not-go' in them. Rachel shrugged her shoulders and gave a sigh. She had no choice.

Lily helped Rachel gather the things Mama had said to take to Mrs. Gunther. As she packed, Lily had some instructions of her own.

"Now, if dat Gun'ter woman ask fo' her boy," Lily warned. "You just tell 'er he gone fishin'."

Rachel jerked back in surprise. "What?"

95

"Mama's who gone mad ovuh chil'uns, just wanna know where dey is," Lily nodded wisely. "Just you tell 'er where he is. It be awright. She be fine."

Now Rachel was really nervous about her task. As she headed down the dirt path too small to be called a road that led past the slave cabins and toward the back fields, she worried about snakes, lizards, and telling lies to a sure enough crazy woman.

It was a beautiful October day. The air was crisp and cool but not uncomfortably so. Rachel normally would've enjoyed a nice, long walk on a fall morning, but, under these circumstances, she yearned to be back in her safe house. Her black leather shoes were already covered in dust as she trudged past the slave cabins, and her arms ached from carrying the overloaded basket of food for Mrs. Gunther.

There was not a sound to be heard except for an occasional warble of a wren. The slave cabins, which were usually bustling with activity, were eerily silent. Everyone, even young mothers with newborn babies strapped to their chests, was required to pick cotton, and the whole area was now abandoned and still. Some of the doors of the cabins were left open, and Rachel could see inside them as she moved past. She stared at the dirt floors and small cots in the one-room houses and felt a strange sense of guilt, like a trespasser in another world. She felt a strong urge to run past and away from these houses, but before she could quicken her pace, an old slave woman unexpectedly stepped out of the last house.

Her skin was dark, rough, and wrinkled, and the sprigs of coarse hair that stuck out from under her head kerchief were white. If Rachel had startled the old woman she did not show it. She didn't even look up at Rachel but walked slowly to a boiling kettle that hung over an open fire and began to stir. Rachel was relieved thinking the old woman had not seen her and hoped she could pass by undetected.

Rachel thought of the stories that Lily and Lizbet had told her about old slave women who could conjure up spells and do other kinds of witchcraft. Rachel wondered if she was a 'conjure woman' and if she was stirring up some kind of brew. Images of owls' heads, cows' tongues, frogs, lizards, and bats came to Rachel's mind as she studied the black kettle. She stepped softly and quickly on the dirt path and held her breath as she got even with the old woman. The woman showed no sign of having seen or heard Rachel.

But, just when Rachel thought she had slipped by unnoticed, the old slave looked up and stared at Rachel. The woman had the blackest eyes Rachel had ever seen, eyes that were like two cold stones. She stared, not *at* Rachel, but *through* her as if she were a ghost. Her icy expression made Rachel shiver and break into a trot to leave the slave houses and the old woman behind.

Once Rachel had gone a safe distance, she slowed back to a walk. She had reached the cotton fields. Here the path ran beside rows and rows of tall cotton plants on one side and very tall willow trees on the other. The sun was warming up, and Rachel could feel small of beads of

sweat forming on her brow, not so much from the heat but from the brisk walking, heavy basket, and nervousness. Everything was still. Rachel felt terribly alone as she walked farther and farther away from her house.

The path turned and ran along the back side of the cotton field. Rachel's house and the slave cabins were now out of sight. All she could see were more rows of cotton and more trees. The pickers were all working in the front forty acres, and for all she knew she was the only person in the whole world right now. If only she could've talked Lizbet into coming along with her. Nothing short of marching her at gunpoint would have been convincing enough. Besides, Lily would never agree to Lizbet leaving the house with so many chores to be done.

Once past the cotton field the path turned again, this time south. It was surrounded on both sides with tall trees whose branches stretched over the path and intertwined so thickly that they blocked out the sun. Long strands of Spanish moss hung down giving everything a ghostly look. Every sound, every movement made Rachel jump. She shivered again. She ached to throw down the basket, turn around, and run home. Mama might not ever find out that Rachel didn't carry out her instructions.

But, Rachel's feet kept walking. She knew she couldn't disappoint her mother. She kept thinking about Mama's words, 'We must be brave,' and she knew she had to see about Mrs. Gunther.

The Gunthers' house was a plain, wooden shack not much bigger than a slave cabin. It sat off the path, down

a slight slope, next to the bayou. Rachel could see the tin roof and brick chimney through the trees. As she got closer to the house her ears and eyes were alert for any signs of life. There were none. Maybe Mrs. Gunther wasn't even at home. Maybe she had gone to look for Henry, too.

Rachel stepped off the path and made her way across the Gunthers' yard. The grass and weeds were almost waist high, and Rachel had to watch carefully where she placed her foot. The bayou was full of creepy, crawling things, and she didn't want to step on anything that moved. Rachel swatted a mosquito on her cheek. Sweat rolled down by her ears along the outline of her jawbone. The hair near her temples was wet; she was breathing hard. If she could just get to the porch steps, she would leave the basket there, turn, and run.

The steps were high, for like most houses built on the banks of water, it was set up off the ground on small brick pillars. Any number of creatures could crawl under the house and be hiding there now, watching her. Rachel forced herself not to look under the porch. One movement in the shadows might send her running.

Rachel stood frozen and listened. There was no sound at all in the house. She was convinced that no one was home, and this boosted her confidence. Feeling very brave now, Rachel ascended the steps to the porch. There she stopped and looked around. The boards of the porch were cracked and rotten. One step might cause the whole thing to collapse beneath her. She took slow, tiny steps and eased carefully to the door.

She waited in front of the door, straining to hear sounds of life inside. All she could hear was the pounding of her own heart. Taking a deep breath, she knocked on the door. Her knock echoed in the silence, startling a crow that was nesting in a nearby tree and causing it to caw and fly away. Rachel jumped at the sudden noise and gasped for breath. She waited again, trying to catch her breath and slow her racing heart. Leaning her ear near the door, she listened again. Nothing happened.

Rachel smiled to herself, let out a sigh of relief, and now feeling braver than ever, knocked one last time. She stepped back and placed the basket near the door.

Just then, the door flew open. Rachel jumped back and screamed. There stood Mrs. Gunther in a ragged cotton dress. Her graying hair was matted and wild. Her cheeks were sunken in, and her eyes, so light blue they were almost gray, had a glazed look. She stared at Rachel in confusion. Rachel stared back with wide, frightened eyes.

"Who are you?" Mrs. Gunther finally said in a heavy German accent.

"I'm Rachel Franklin, ma'am," Rachel stammered. "I've... I've brought . . ."

"You know my Henrich?" she asked again. "You are a frient?"

Rachel did not know how to answer. Yes, she knew Henry, but no, she was not a friend.

"Please, please," Mrs. Gunther held onto Rachel with one hand and motioned to a chair with the other. "Please... come... sit."

Rachel looked around the small room. She had never seen such filth in all her life. Rotten food, dirty clothes, and the smell, the wretched smell made it almost impossible to breathe. All Rachel wanted to do was put down the basket and get out. But there was no place to put it. What little furniture there was in the room was covered with trash and tools and Lord-knows-what.

Mrs. Gunther kept insisting that Rachel sit down, but there was no empty chair. She finally led Rachel to a small bed in the corner. She threw some clothes and trash off the bed onto the floor and cleared Rachel a spot on which to sit. Reluctantly, Rachel sat on the very edge of the bed, keeping her hands on the basket.

"Please, can you tell me," Mrs. Gunther's voice was urgent, and her eyes were pleading. "Can you tell me where ist my boy Henrich?"

Rachel was in a dilemma. She didn't know where Henry was except he had gone off to the war. She remembered what Lily had told her, but it seemed such a silly thing to say. Besides, it was a lie to say he had gone fishing, and Rachel knew better than to tell a lie.

But Mrs. Gunther was working herself up into a frenzy, wringing her hands and grabbing Rachel by the arms. Her eyes were round and wild. Her hair stuck out like

tiny snakes and seemed to grow each time she shook her head. She kept asking the question over and over, gripping Rachel harder until she was shaking Rachel furiously.

Frightened, Rachel struggled to free herself from the mad woman's grasp. She finally broke loose, dropped the basket on the floor, and made for the door. Mrs. Gunther began to weep, collapsing on her knees and burying her face in the bed where Rachel had just escaped. Her cries were so pitiful that instead of racing out the door, Rachel stopped and said,

"Mrs. Gunther, Henry's gone fishin'."

Much to Rachel's disbelief, the sobbing woman suddenly stopped crying and turned to look at Rachel. There was a stunned looked on her face and her eyes brightened.

"Yah, I t'ink you are right," she wiped her face with a dirty handkerchief. "Henrich ist fishink."

Then Mrs. Gunther laughed. It was a nervous, witch-like laugh that sent chills up Rachel's spine.

Rachel waited no longer. She was out the door and down the steps, running as if the devil himself were chasing her. But even as she reached the path, she could still hear Mrs. Gunther talking and laughing hysterically to herself.

For weeks the nightmare wouldn't stop. Every night Rachel dreamed of faces with cold black eyes and wild gray ones, witches and snakes that squeezed the breath out of you, storms that blew you off your feet, hands that grabbed, pulled, and shook you. Many mornings Rachel awoke to find herself sleeping on Mama's bed.

Then the fever hit. For three days Rachel tossed and moaned and slept. Mama or Lily stayed by her bed day and night, putting cool, damp cloths on her forehead, lifting her up to sip broth from a cup. Fever was a serious matter. Dr. Prentiss was called in. Shaking his head he confessed he didn't know as yet what the ailment was. Nothing was going around in the county except a few cases of whooping cough and the 'misery.' He promised to check on Rachel in a couple of days unless her condition worsened, in which case, he urged them to send for him pronto.

Finally on the fourth day, Rachel's fever broke. She sat up and looked around.

"I'm hungry," she proclaimed.

Lily jumped up from her chair beside the bed.

"Law-w-sy, chile!" she exclaimed. Lily pressed her hand to Rachel's forehead. It felt cool and dry. "Da fevuh done broke. Praise da Lord!"

Then Lily whirled around and left the room. Rachel heard her calling Mama and giving orders to Jo and Mott as she scampered down the stairs. Soon there was a tray of warm food on Rachel's lap, and she dug in. Mama and Lily smiled as they watched her devour the food.

Somehow, during this fitful time of nightmares and fever, October turned into November. The days were pleasantly cool, and the nights were down-right chilly. The slaves were almost finished with their last round of picking cotton, and everyone was busy preparing for winter. Mama was in good spirits because Mr. Gunther had miraculously returned with Henry in tow. Whether or not Henry would stay at home was another matter (Lily guessed he'd be gone by spring), but Mama didn't care. Mr. Gunther was here now and would take the burdens off Mama's shoulders.

The first frost arrived on a Tuesday, the twelfth of November. Rachel looked out her window and marveled at the icy sparkles that covered the ground, the trees, the barn roof, everything. The light of the rising sun made everything shimmer. She smiled. This was a good day, a happy day. It was Rachel's birthday, and she was turning eleven years old.

She knew the celebration would be much quieter than in years past. With the Franklin men still off to war, no one felt like celebrating anything, but she knew there would be cake and, hopefully, a present or two. Mama had invited several of her friends from neighboring farms to stop by in the afternoon. This was a rare treat, and she was excited about it.

Rachel scurried to put on her slippers and robe. Her room was freezing, and she was anxious to get to the warm kitchen. Usually she dressed before going downstairs, but today she was up exceptionally early, and it was just too cold to get dressed. Besides, she was near starving for breakfast.

As Rachel entered the kitchen Lily was putting a batch of warm biscuits on the table. Behind her was Lizbet car-

105

rying a pan of fried bacon in one hand and a bowl of gravy in the other. Rachel was watching the two of them and the food so closely that she didn't see the two packages on the floor.

"Well, ain't you gone open 'em?" Lizbet pointed to a small wooden crate and a bundle that was wrapped in oilcloth and tied with heavy twine.

"That's for me?" Rachel asked in disbelief. She had never received a package before, much less, two.

"It yo' birt'day, ain't it?" Lily butted in, sounding a little annoyed.

"Open 'em, plea-ea-se," begged Lizbet. Her eyes were round with excitement. "I been waitin' two whole days."

Rachel stared at Lizbet, still in disbelief, not so much that the packages had arrived without her knowledge but that Lizbet had been able to keep it a secret for two whole days. She forgot about breakfast and moved to examine the packages more closely.

"Where's Mama?" she asked, not wanting to disturb anything without Mama's permission.

"She in da study lookin' at some papers," Lily answered. "She be done d'rectly. It time to eat an' she be smellin' dees biscuits."

Rachel looked at the packages again, then at Lizbet who was urging her with all the facial expression she could muster to open the packages.

Lily pointed to the small bundle. "Dat dere's from Missuh William."

Lizbet was nodding her head furiously.

Rachel picked it up. It was small but very heavy. She was about to burst herself to see what was in it. So she yanked and tugged on the twine. It wouldn't be broken or untied. Lily reached for a butcher knife and, in one jerk, cut the heavy cord.

With their heads together Rachel and Lizbet pulled open the stiff oilcloth and uncovered a bolt of the most beautiful blue velvet material Rachel had ever seen. She lifted it up, and packed underneath was a spool of delicate, white lace, ribbons, and a mother-of-pearl hair comb. Rachel's mouth flew open, and she sucked in a big breath of surprise.

"Oh, dear, how beautiful!" Mama said as she entered the kitchen. "Papa wanted you to have a new Christmas dress. This'll make a beautiful one."

Mama lifted up the material.

"You know, hon'," Mama added, "this material was very hard to come by. With the blockade, goods like this are becoming scarce. I don't know how your Papa was able to get it."

They smiled at each other.

"I'm awfully glad he did," Rachel said.

"Me, too," Mama replied, folding the cloth ever so gently and laying it back with the lace and the comb.

"Can I open this one, Mama?" Rachel asked excitedly, pointing to the wooden box.

"Of course, dear, it's from Bud."

Rachel studied the crate, wondering how to get into it. She didn't have long to wonder for Lily appeared with

107

an iron bar. She began to pry off the wooden slats from the top. Then Rachel and Lizbet each grabbed handfuls of the straw that protected whatever treasure was packed inside. At the same time their hands reached a smaller box, and together they lifted it out of the crate. This, too, was tied with twine, and again Lily was quick with her knife to snap the string loose.

Rachel held her breath as she lifted the lid. She stared into the box only a split second, but that was too long for Lizbet.

"What in dere?" she asked eagerly. "What in dere?"

"Look," was all Rachel could say. When she turned the box toward Lizbet, Mama and Lily both bent down to take a look, too.

There inside was a beautiful silver box with a miniature man and woman standing on the top. The man had black hair and a moustache. He was wearing a black, frock-tail coat. The woman also had black hair that was long and curly and hung down her back. Even though she was no bigger than Rachel's little finger, all the details of her face were vivid, blue eyes and red lips. She was wearing a white gown and white gloves that went up to her elbows. The couple was posed as if dancing a waltz. Rachel lifted the small box right up to her eyes. She studied the faces of the tiny pair and decided immediately that they were in love. She examined every tiny feature from their hands down to their feet.

"Look, Rachel," Mama was pointing at a small knob on the side of the silver box. "It's a music box. Wind it up."

Rachel set the music box on the table and very slowly turned the knob. She turned it until it stopped, and as soon as she let go, music began to play as the couple on top began to turn. Lizbet gasped. Even Lily, who rarely showed any emotion at all, let out a cry of surprise. It was like nothing they had ever seen before.

Rachel could've watched that pretty couple dance all day. But there was more in the crate from Bud. Rachel let the music box play, for Lily and Lizbet couldn't take their eyes off it, as she dug in the straw again. There she found another package wrapped in brown paper and tied with string. She easily untied this one. Seashells. Bud had sent her all sorts of seashells, small ones that looked like a fan, bigger ones like cones. He had included a note with the shells.

It read: *Put the conch shell to your ear and listen. You will hear the ocean.*

Rachel handed the note to Mama. She read it and then pointed to the biggest cone-shaped shell.

"This one's the conch, dear," Mama said.

"Will I really hear the ocean?" asked Rachel.

Mama smiled and nodded.

Rachel placed the conch shell over her ear and waited. Her eyes got big, and she began to smile. Then she laughed.

"I can hear it!" she exclaimed. "I can. I can hear the ocean."

Then she passed her conch shell around to Mama, Lily, and Lizbet. All were laughing as they finally sat

down to eat breakfast. Rachel checked her wooden crate one last time to see if all the presents had been found. She dug around in the straw and, much to her delight, found a letter from Bud. She would not read it now but wait until after breakfast. Then she would find a quiet place and enjoy it all by herself.

By the fireplace in the parlor was the only choice for reading. Most of the other rooms, her room especially, were too cold. So Rachel curled up on the sofa and began to read:

Dear Rachel,

I hope you are having a happy birthday. It's hard to believe that 11 years have passed since you were a crying baby. I remember well the crying. But now, you're a growing young lady. Pretty soon Papa and I will have to scare all the young beaus away from our porch.

I hope you like the music box. I thought of you as soon as I saw the beautiful lady. I think you will look just like her when you are grown except more beautiful. The shells I gathered from the shore near Mobile one day when I was on an outing. They do let us get away from camp sometimes.

I have visited New Orleans on several occasions. If you will keep this secret from Mama I will tell you that I bought a strange doll for you there. It was stuffed with real human hair and dressed in a strange robe.

Its hair was wild like a lion's mane. I was told it was a voo-doo doll used to put hexes on people. I decided it would be wiser not to send the doll to you as it might upset our mother or Lily or both. Rather, I will put a blue uniform on it and put hexes on the Yankees!

Give my love to Mama. I promise to be home for Christmas.

All my love,

Bud

P.S. I still have your blue ribbon.

Rachel read the letter three times before putting it away. She would not share it with Mama, even though Mama read all her letters out loud. This was her special letter and, besides, it had a secret in it. But she would share the good news. Rachel ran to tell Mama that Bud was coming home for Christmas.

Little did Rachel know, that was not the only good news to arrive on her birthday.

8

'Tis the Season

november, 186

THE SUN WAS LOW IN THE SKY when the last of the birthday guests said their farewells. A large, autumn moon, perfectly round and bright orange, was on the rise, lighting the roads for their journey home. Mama and Rachel relaxed by the parlor fireplace as the temperature dropped outside. The tinkling sound of Rachel's music box and the crackle of the fire were the only sounds to be heard.

Rachel's eyes were glued to the miniature dancers as she thought about the day and wondered about life as an eleven-year-old. Mama hummed contentedly as she worked on her sewing. Christmas was just around the corner, the Franklin men would be home soon, and life was good.

But the serenity didn't last long. Sounds of a distant rider disturbed their peacefulness. Mama and Rachel both listened, waiting to hear if the rider was coming closer. Mama's shoulder tensed, and she dropped her needlework in her lap. The galloping hooves got louder and louder until the rider was at the porch. Rachel watched Mama anxiously as they heard footsteps pound across the porch. Mama rose quickly and was at the door as the first knock came.

Rachel stood behind Mama as she squared her shoulders, took a deep breath, and slowly opened the door. The messenger was just a young boy, not much older than herself, Rachel guessed. He appeared to take his job very seriously and, acting as if he were of great importance himself, snapped to attention and quickly produced a telegram from his pouch.

Mama took the paper and thanked the boy without so much as glancing down at the telegram. She offered him supper 'round back, but the boy declined. He had more messages to deliver and emphasized the urgency at which he worked. He turned, leaped onto his horse, and was off in a flash.

Mama closed the door quickly against the cold evening air. But still she did not look at the paper in her hand. She looked at Rachel, and her pretty green eyes were moist. They held hands as they sat down again in front of the fireplace. Only then did Mama acknowledge the telegram.

She opened it slowly and read it to herself. Suddenly, her mouth flew open, and she covered her lips with her

114

hand. 'Oh, my!' was all she could say. Rachel was searching Mama's face frantically, and when she saw a tiny tear roll down the corner of her mother's eye she exclaimed,

"What is it, Mama?"

Mama looked up. Her eyes glistened. "It's a boy!"

There were lots of things Rachel expected to hear, but this was not one of them, and for a few seconds she was totally confused.

"Laura Millbrook's had her baby," Mama said through tears of joy. "It's a boy. Six pounds six ounces. He was born two days ago. His name is John Evan Millbrook III."

Rachel jumped, squealed, and clapped her hands.

"Oh, Mama, can we go see him?" she begged. "Plea-ea-se can we?"

Mama laughed at Rachel's excitement. She thought a minute and let out a big sigh. "I wish we could, dear. I don't know. I'll have to think about it." Then she looked at the telegram again and smiled. "A little boy," she said softly to herself.

The next morning Rachel jumped out of bed and looked out her window, expecting to see Josup preparing the carriage for the trip to the Millbrook estate. But much to her disappointment, there was no Josup, no carriage, no suitcases, and no lunch basket.

"I know you're disappointed, hon'. I am too," Mama explained over breakfast. "But I don't feel right about leaving just now, what with so much to be done around here."

"But, Mama, Mr. Gunther's back," Rachel pleaded. "Can't he look after things?"

"Yes, I know he's back," Mama sighed. "But I'm not so sure that boy won't run away again, and then off goes Mr. Gunther again. Besides, the weather is awfully cold, and a long ride might bring on your fever again."

Rachel wanted to stomp her feet and pout. But she was now eleven years old and much too old for tantrums. Instead, she let her bottom lip pooch out, and her eyes droop sadly. She knew Mama wanted to see the new baby even more than she did. She wanted Mama to feel just badly enough to change her mind. But nothing worked this time. Mama had toughened a lot over the last months, and the responsibility of the plantation was more impor- tant than an outing to see Miss Laura and the baby.

"Maybe over the holidays," Mama promised. "Maybe Papa will drive us." She kissed Rachel on the top of her head. "I'm sure we'll see the baby soon."

Rachel certainly hoped she would get to see him while he was still a baby, and she started to say as much. But, she knew it would do no good to continue to fuss. The discussion about the trip and the baby was over. Mama had made up her mind.

There was so much to do for the holidays that time seemed to fly by. War or no war there would still be Christmas, and that meant dinners to be planned, pres- ents to be made, and a new blue velvet dress to be sewn. Mama worked tirelessly on the dress. Rachel did her part, trying on and standing still for countless fittings while Mama pinned, measured, pinned some more, and measured again. Rachel was sure to have the prettiest dress in the whole county.

Usually Christmas meant a trip to Jackson where the family stayed at the finest hotel, attending parties and having dinner with friends. Their trip might last two, even three, weeks. But this year, because Papa and Bud had been away from home for so long and because they never knew when they would be unexpectedly called away, the Franklins had decided to stay home. They would have their own Christmas dinner party to celebrate the return of the men. Mama and Rachel were busy with the preparations, cleaning, decorating, planning the food, and inviting guests. December had arrived, and every day was filled with too much to do.

Yes, Christmas was coming. But, by the same token, there was still a war going on. Even though there had been little or no fighting in the last months, there were many things to be done for the Cause. The ladies continued to meet at least once a week to knit socks, sew shirts and pants, and tear bandages. Today the sewing group was meeting in Rachel's parlor. So many quick, busy fingers, so much chit-chatting. Miss Rosalee Prentiss, who had no children of her own and no husband in the war, seemed, nonetheless, to always be the authority on subjects of the war and babies and everything else. At the moment, Rachel and all the other ladies were listening to her up-date on how the war was progressing.

"Why, anyone can see which side has the fightin' men," she declared loudly. "Those Yankees won't even come out

of hiding. Hmph!" she snorted. "The North with all their big talk of 'Little Mac'... what's he done? Nothing... just a lot of puffed up struttin' around. Can't get him into a fight no more than a stubborn mule, I say. Our boys are the real fighters. And they'll lick the Yankees again next go-round."

All the ladies nodded in agreement. Some sighed, and others simply sewed faster and harder, thinking about their husbands, brothers, or sons who would have to do that fighting. Thank goodness someone changed the subject to the new Millbrook baby.

"Oh, I bet he's a darlin'," bubbled Mrs. Lurleen Adams who had a nine-month-old infant herself and two older children besides. Her husband was somewhere in Virginia.

"He'll be a handsome lad," another chimed in.

Of course, Miss Rosalee snatched away the conversation once again.

"Oh, he's a fine one, I'm sure," she commented. "He would have to be with such a pretty mother and handsome father."

Everyone again nodded in agreement. The ladies were smiling just thinking about a new baby. But Miss Rosalee didn't stop there.

"God does have a way of givin' back what He takes away," she said, never looking up from her sewing. Rachel believed even if all the ladies left the room, Miss Rosalee would still be talking for all she was worth. "I mean, with so many men killed already on the battlefield and so many more to be killed before the war is over, we need sons to be born. We'll near run out of men folk if we don't birth lots of boy babies."

Once again, Miss Rosalee had managed to cause wives and mothers to think about the danger to their beloved men. Smiles disappeared, and faces dropped. Everyone again became totally absorbed in her needle-work. Mama let out an audible sigh and quickly left the room for refreshments. Rachel seized the chance to leave and followed Mama out of the room. She could hear Miss Rosalee's voice all the way down the hall.

A warm cup of apple cider and a piece of gingerbread can do wonders for lifting spirits, and it was just what the sewing group needed. Mama had come to the rescue, and for the moment, at least, Miss Rosalee was silenced. It is nearly impossible to dominate the conversation with one's mouth full. Soon the ladies were chit-chatting again about Christmas and parties, laughing softly and smiling.

They were so engrossed in their light conversation that no one heard the door open or saw the two visitors standing in the hallway. Several minutes passed as the ladies talked and sipped on cider. Finally someone looked up and gasped,

"Belle! Oh, praise the Lord!"

Mama looked toward the hall and dropped her cup. She clasped her hands to her throat and stood up. She couldn't speak or even breathe.

There stood Papa, and beside him was a tall man with a black moustache, almost a mirror image of Papa.

Rachel stared at the stranger until she realized it was Bud. Mama ran to them and wrapped her arms around both of her men. They embraced her as well, Papa kissing Mama's hair and Bud burying his face in the curve of her neck. For a few seconds everyone froze, not wanting to interrupt this tender homecoming. Some ladies began to sniff, and others wiped their eyes with their handkerchiefs. Then Mama looked up at Bud. She cupped her hands around his face and studied it as tears ran down her cheeks. Rachel watched from the parlor, too stunned to move.

Then Bud strode into the room, and with all the ladies' eyes glued to him in amazement, he lifted Rachel off the floor and hugged her tightly. It was really Bud. He had finally come home, and Rachel could hardly believe it. She wrapped her arms around his neck and hugged him with all her might.

Suddenly, the room was aflutter. The sewing group began to quickly gather their things and call for their drivers. All the ladies, even Miss Rosalee, knew it was not a time for guests, but a time for being alone. Not only that, seeing the Franklin men come home gave them all hope that their men might be home as well, and everyone was anxious to get there and see.

When the house was empty of guests the Franklins sat together in the parlor. They were a family again, and there was so much to talk about. Mama and Rachel were a good audience for Bud, laughing at his stories about the men in his camp, sympathizing over his hardships, and

being duly thrilled at his tales of adventure. Bud was careful not to tell stories about any real danger for fear of worrying his mother and sister. Papa was unusually quiet as he watched his family, absorbed in the faces he had not seen in such a long time.

The afternoon passed quickly, and it was soon time to freshen up for supper. Rachel didn't want to leave her brother's side, but, much to her surprise, Bud excused himself first and was off on his horse.

"Where's he goin', Mama?" she asked in dismay.

"I think he has a little business to attend to," was all Mama would say. "He'll be back shortly." Mama smiled and then insisted Rachel go to her room and get ready for supper.

Papa, Mama, and Rachel sat at the dining table and watched Jo and Mott put dishes of hot food on the table. Bud was not back yet, and Rachel was annoyed and confused. What in the world could be so important that he had to leave so soon after just arriving. She was about to express her irritation when the front door opened, and she found out what was so important.

Suzanna Wade.

Now Rachel was really annoyed and confused. She couldn't believe Bud would bring a silly girl to dinner on his first night at home. Everything was ruined, and Rachel began to scowl. She had certainly lost her appetite.

Mama jumped up to greet Suzanna. Mama was always a gracious hostess, but the glow on her face showed that she was genuinely glad to see their unexpected guest.

They embraced, and Mama continued to wrap her arm around Suzanna's waist as she led her into the dining room. Papa stood up as Suzanna entered the room, and Bud quickly stepped ahead to pull her chair out for her. This made Rachel scowl even more to see everyone acting so silly over an even sillier girl.

All through dinner Bud didn't seem to take his eyes off Suzanna. Occasionally their eyes met, and she would smile and blush. In fact, she was the center of everyone's attention, and Rachel felt sick. She wanted to excuse herself from the table, but she knew Mama would scold her afterwards for showing such bad manners. So Rachel picked at her food and pretended to be listening.

She didn't care if Suzanna had a pretty smile or that she was trying hard to include Rachel in the conversation. She didn't want Suzanna to be this nice. Rachel was trying hard not to like Suzanna, this intruder on their family, but it was becoming increasingly harder not to smile back when she spoke so sweetly to Rachel. So Rachel finally excused herself from the table and disappeared to her room. She fell asleep wishing that Suzanna Wade would go away and never come back.

But, she did come back. She was a regular at all their evening meals for the next week. Bud was supposed to be spending time with his family, and Rachel was furious every time Suzanna butted in. She couldn't understand why Bud was letting Suzanna share in their family time.

"Mama, why does that ol' Suzanna Wade come here

so much?" Rachel blurted out one day. She was about ready to burst with frustration.

"She's a good friend of Bud's, dear," Mama said quietly. "I guess you would call them sweethearts."

Rachel made a face. She felt mad and hurt and sick all at the same time to think her brother had a sweetheart. Mama glanced up to see the scowling face and added,

"You'll understand someday when you're older."

Rachel doubted if she'd ever understand Bud and Suzanna Wade. She hoped he'd soon come to his senses and be the *old* Bud again, the one who only liked to hunt and ride horses and play games with her. But Rachel would soon learn that life in her family was going to be different. It happened at their big Christmas party.

The Franklin house had never looked so bright and festive. Papa and Bud had cut down a huge Christmas tree, and they had all worked to decorate it. There were wreaths of evergreen on the doors and windows, and evergreen rope with pretty red bows entwined the staircase. Every lamp and candle was lit making the rooms sparkle. Laughter filled the air. For at least one night there would be no talk of war—Mama insisted on it—and every guest was in a cheerful, holiday mood.

Rachel was simply beautiful in her new dress. The finishing touches had been done just in time, and Papa beamed when he saw his little girl. Bud had teased her about all the beaus she would have when the young boys saw her. Mary Beth O'Connor, who was thirteen and loved to flaunt her new clothes, turned almost green with envy. The handful of other girls Rachel's age who were at the party clustered around her, touching the soft velvet and 'oohing' in admiration.

Lily, Jo, Mott, and even Lizbet were dressed in crisp gingham dresses and white aprons as they busily covered the tables with dishes of steaming food. The four of them had bustled around like bees for days preparing the food: roast goose, baked ham, vegetables of all kinds, sweet breads, and cakes. There was even a tray of oranges, lemons, and dates, a rare treat, especially with the blockade in operation. Papa had somehow managed to get his hands on the precious fruits and paid an outrageous price. But Papa said it was a very special night and well worth it.

A special night... Rachel had heard it said hundreds of times in the past week. Mama had wanted nothing but the best, and Papa had spared no expense. Every piece of silverware, every doorknob, every window had been cleaned till it sparkled. The Franklins had given holiday parties before, and Rachel didn't really understand why this one was particularly special. But she soon found out.

Tink! Tink! Tink! Papa rapped his spoon on his glass. Everyone hushed, and all eyes turned toward the end of the table where Papa stood. His dark blue eyes were glistening as he cleared his throat and began to speak. He spoke of the joys of being home and seeing old friends. There were nods of agreement as he talked of the strength of the South and its people.

Then he did something very unusual. He invited Bud and Suzanna Wade to stand at the head of the table with him. Rachel quickly looked to her mother for an explanation, but she, too, had joined Papa at his side.

"I have a very important announcement to make," Papa said proudly. "Our Bud has asked Miss Suzanna Wade for her hand in marriage."

Rachel's mouth flew open. She stared at Bud, then at Papa and Mama, and finally at Suzanna. They were all smiling. Why hadn't somebody told her? She was the only one left out of the secret. Her face turned red, and she fought back tears.

Papa raised his glass, and all in the room lifted their glasses as well. He made a toast, but Rachel didn't hear it. She was still in shock over the surprise news, and her ears were ringing. She was glad everyone was too busy drinking a toast to the newly betrothed couple to notice that she was dizzy and about to faint. She started to sit down when Papa called her to him. All eyes turned to the little girl in the blue velvet dress as Rachel tried to smile and move her feet. Mama quickly made her way to the back of the room where Rachel was standing with the other children and led her to the front. There she stood between her father and her future sister-in-law as all the guests moved to congratulate the family.

Ladies dabbed their eyes. Such a beautiful couple! Men slapped Bud on the back. Lucky man! They shook Papa's hand. You must be so proud! And hugged Mama.

She's a lovely girl, Belle! So many questions about the wedding plans, so many suggestions, so much advice! Rachel was sure she was going to be sick or faint or both. All she wanted to do was go to her room, and at the first opportunity, when no one was looking, that's just what she did.

Rachel threw herself across her bed and lay there thinking in the dark. Hearing the noise from downstairs, she felt as though she was the only one in the whole world who was miserable. She didn't want Bud and Suzanna to get married. She didn't want her brother to live in another house. She didn't want her family to change. Rachel began to sob.

Just then, there was a soft knock on the door. Rachel sat up and wiped her eyes. She was sure it was Mama come to scold her or Papa to see if she was really sick. Or even Lily to demand she get herse'f back down dem stairs. But when she said, "Who is it?" she got a big surprise.

"It's me, Suzanna," a soft voice answered.

Rachel jumped up, frantically wiped her face, and smoothed her dress. She hated for Suzanna to find her in her room in the dark, but there was no candle, and she knew she must open the door or else be scolded by her parents and Bud for being rude.

There stood Suzanna with a lamp in her hand.

"Are you feeling all right, Rachel?" she asked with genuine concern. "May I come in?"

Rachel stepped back and opened the door wider. It was an unspoken invitation to enter her room.

"I hope you're not coming down with something," she continued. "It would be such a shame to be sick on Christmas."

"No," Rachel finally spoke up. Suzanna was being so sweet Rachel couldn't ignore her for long. "No, I'm not sick. Just too many people. I needed to lie down."

"Well, I just had to speak to you. Isn't it wonderful that we're going to be sisters?" Suzanna was excited now. "I've never had a sister, and I think it'll be fun."

Rachel thought about this for a minute. Of course, she'd never had a sister either, and she'd never really thought what it would be like to have one. Rachel began to warm to the idea.

"Oh, we can do so many things together," Suzanna giggled. "I know you play the piano. Well, I do too. We could play together sometime. And go riding in the afternoons. And when this awful war is over, we can go to Jackson and have tea at Anderton's. Won't it be just grand? To be sisters, I mean."

Suzanna was so full of excitement that Rachel couldn't help but be excited, too. She smiled at Suzanna, and they held hands for a minute.

"We have so much to do before the wedding," Suzanna began to bubble again. "I want you to see the material for my wedding dress. It was terribly hard to get our hands on such nice fabric, such as the way things are now. There's hardly a bolt of fine linen or satin anywhere in the state. The dress hasn't even been started yet, of course... this being rather sudden and all… but it's going to be beautiful. Bud and I thought we'd be married in the spring, but with the war… well, everything is so uncertain, we decided to do it before he leaves. Sometime at the end of January. A winter wedding is really nice, don't you think?"

Suzanna finally stopped to catch her breath. Her face showed how truly happy she was, and it made Rachel happy, too. Suzanna took her hand again.

"Are you happy about the wedding, Rachel?" she asked but didn't wait for an answer. "Bud and I want you to be happy. He loves you so. He wants you to be as happy as we are. You are happy, aren't you, Rachel?"

Rachel nodded. There was only one thing she could possibly say,

"Of course, I'm happy."

Suzanna quickly stood up. "Good. I knew you'd be happy for us."

She went to the door leaving Rachel in the dark again. Then Suzanna quickly spun around.

"We'll have such fun being sisters, just you wait and see."

Then she was off down the stairs and back to all the well-wishers. Rachel smiled to herself. She did feel better. Maybe having Suzanna Wade in the family was not such a bad thing. Maybe it would be fun.

As every day passed Rachel discovered that it was fun being with Suzanna. She was already very much a part of their family, and she was there nearly all the time. One reason for this was Suzanna's own home life. She lived alone with her mother who was weak and sickly and rarely left the house. Her father had been killed years ago in a riding accident when Suzanna was just a little girl. He had been a banker and had left Suzanna and her mother a big house in town with plenty of money on which to live. There was an uncle who looked after them but no brothers or sisters to keep Suzanna company.

Rachel remembered Suzanna's excitement about being 'sisters,' and she had to admit it was wonderful. Suzanna helped Rachel with her sewing. They played duets on the piano and read their favorite stories to each other. They giggled whenever Suzanna showed Rachel how to flirt, batting her eyelids and offering her hand with wrist arched high. After supper, they played games with Bud, and it made him laugh just to see his 'girls' getting along so well.

But, no matter what the conversation was, it never strayed long from talk of the wedding. It was the focus of everyone's attention. The date had been set for January 19, a Sunday afternoon. That would give the newly married couple a week to honeymoon in New Orleans before Bud would report back to his camp sometime in early February. Plans were constantly being made and changed, work on the wedding dress kept all female hands busy, and preparations for the wedding party was everyone's concern. Christmas morning came and went, and although it was very special as always, minds quickly returned to the upcoming event.

Mama fretted over just about everything, or rather, the lack of everything. No silk to be had for new dresses.

No new hats or shoes. All would have to make do with what they already had, which would've been unthinkable before the war. Food for the wedding guests was a major problem as prices on even the basics, flour, sugar, and salt, had soared sky-high. All delicacies and luxuries were becoming impossible to obtain at any price. What special foods Papa had managed to get for the Christmas party seemed out of his power to get now.

But Mama was determined that Bud and Suzanna's wedding would be perfect, and everyone was jumping to please her. Bud teased that she was worse than any general he had encountered so far in the war. But even the best of generals, or mothers, can't control everything. Certainly not the war.

The dispatch arrived the day after Christmas regardless of Mama's plans. Papa read it to himself. His brow wrinkled, and his blue eyes grew dark. Without a word he handed it to Bud who also read it silently and reacted likewise. It was an order of great urgency for Bud to report back to his camp within a week. Mama was incredulous.

"What could possibly be so important that you have to leave before February?" she demanded to know.

"Confederate forces are forming a line of defense across southern Kentucky to protect northern Tennessee," replied Bud as calmly as he could speak in hopes of calming his mother. "The Union army is threatening an advance in this area. General Albert Johnston is calling for all troops to fortify the defense."

"But, Bud, the wedding…" Mama looked to Papa for an answer to this sudden catastrophe. There was nothing Papa nor Bud could do. Orders were orders. Mama knew it as well as the men, but she needed to protest to show her deep disappointment. "This is awful… just awful. Oh, poor Suzanna. Her heart will be broken."

Mama began to sniff and wipe back tears of frustration. She knew Bud felt terrible, too, but she couldn't control her emotions. Papa came to her rescue, wrapped his arms around her shoulders, and let her sob into his coat.

"I need to see Suzanna," was all Bud said as he grabbed his heavy overcoat and headed out the door. Minutes later he had Lightning saddled and was off down the lane.

Rachel thought someone had died when she came downstairs for supper. Papa was solemn-faced. Mama's green eyes were red and swollen from crying. And Bud was nowhere to be seen.

"What's happened, Papa?" Rachel asked, afraid to approach her grieving mother.

Papa looked at Rachel and sighed, "Come here."

Rachel walked to Papa, and just as he had done when she was much younger, he lifted her up and put her on his lap. He always smoothed her hair back from her face and stroked the long curls down her back.

"Bud's been called back," he finally answered.

Rachel's eyes got big with surprise. "When? Today?"

Papa chuckled softly but not happily. "No, hon'. Not today. But soon. In a few days."

"But, Papa, what about the wedding? Can't Bud and Suzanna get married anymore?" Rachel was about to cry herself.

"I don't know, dear," Papa said. "I just don't know. That'll be up to Bud and Suzanna."

So the clock ticked on as they waited in the parlor for Bud to return. There couldn't have been a more melancholy threesome, Mama still wiping her eyes, Papa staring blankly into the fire, and Rachel moping with disappointment. This war was ruining everything.

Finally a buggy approached. Rachel ran to look out the window.

"They're here!" Rachel almost screamed.

Bud had driven Suzanna in her buggy with Lightning tied to the back. The couple came in shivering from the cold. They quickly took off their coats and stepped into the parlor. Holding hands, they were breathing hard from the brisk walk or from the cold wind or was it excitement? Papa, Mama, and Rachel held their breaths as they watched the two and waited.

"We've decided to get married before I go," Bud announced with a big smile on his face. He looked at his bride-to-be, and they both grinned.

Mama was stunned. She was thinking of all the plans that had been made and all the preparations that would have to be done in little time.

"When?" was all she said so softly that no one even heard.

Bud was talking to Papa, and Suzanna was chattering to Rachel. Then they all stopped and turned their attention to Mama. She was still in shock.

Suzanna spoke up first. "Mrs. Franklin, we're going to be married in three days. Don't worry. Everything'll be fine."

Mama just nodded her head.

And in three days Bud and Suzanna stood before Reverend Mitchell in the parlor. Suzanna was beautiful in Mama's altered wedding gown. The new gown was yet unfinished and now never would be. Her soft, brown curls were hidden by the long lace veil that had once been her mother's. The train of her dress flowed around her feet as she stood by Bud's side.

Bud was tall, slim, and handsome in his gray officer's uniform. Rachel liked this uniform even better than his academy one. The collar had a single gold bar to show his rank of second lieutenant. There was gold braiding on his sleeve sewn in a most unique design of circles and loops. This also designated his rank. Bud had explained all the different uniforms for different ranking officers, but Rachel hadn't really cared to pay attention. She just thought his uniform was pretty with the light blue on gray and all the gold buttons.

Rachel sat between Mama and Papa as the preacher recited the vows. Suzanna's mother sat close to the fire. She had managed to make the short buggy ride from town with the help of Suzanna's Uncle Phillip who had walked Suzanna to the altar in her father's place. Mrs. Wade's face was terribly pale and sunken in. She seemed hardly able to sit up, and Rachel was afraid she might faint right in the middle of the ceremony.

The wedding was short, but simply beautiful, as Mama said later. There was a fine supper afterwards for the two small families who had just been united and Reverend Mitchell. These few guests left soon after the meal, Mrs. Wade feeling too sickly to sit longer and the reverend, having performed his duty and filled his stomach, ready to get home. The newly married couple left, too. Since they would not get a honeymoon trip to New Orleans, they would at least get a night alone together. Bud had secured a room at the only decent hotel in town, The Clairmont, for one night. And so in a flurry of hugs and kisses, waves and sniffles, the new Mr. and Mrs. Franklin departed.

By the dawning of the new year both Franklin men would be gone once more to war. No one could predict what the year 1862 would bring. Hopes were high that the war would end before the year would. One fact would be apparent very soon. In 1862 the war would heat up, and it would not cool off for three and a half long, bloody years.

9

A Ghost Comes to Call

april, 1862

WAR IS CRUEL AND UNMERCIFUL. It kills men. It destroys homes and families. It breaks men but, strangely enough, it makes men, too. War can transform ordinary men into heroes in one brief moment of bravery, in a single act of courage. Great leaders can emerge from the ranks of common men through their strength of character and deeds of valor. This was never truer than in the War Between the States since so many ordinary men—farmers, tailors, merchants, teachers, and even clergy—took up arms. Names that were destined to die with the human forms that bore them became, instead, names that lived on in history. One such name that began to rise to fame in 1862 was Ulysses S. Grant.

Grant was considered a failure in civilian life. The southern people called him a 'drunk' and claimed he wouldn't last six months under the pressure of generalship. Grant had been forced to resign a captain's commission in California some years back due to fondness of the 'bottle.' Northerners weren't sure about his stability as a leader either, but for the time he was the only general who was taking action, and action is what they needed. George McClellan was proving to be a great disappointment in Virginia, not having moved his army since given his command at least nine months back. He seemed to be mired in the training and recruiting of troops, and nothing, not even the President himself, was able to spur him into a fight.

Grant, on the other hand, had been very busy in the last few months. Under his command, the United States flag was raised over Tennessee for the first time since the state had seceded from the Union. It happened first at Fort Henry on the Tennessee River, then at Fort Donelson on the Cumberland River. These two rivers come together west of Nashville, capital city of Tennessee, and run parallel up through Kentucky to the Ohio River. The forts were built hurriedly by the Confederates to protect entrance into Tennessee from the North and also to help fortify General Albert Sidney Johnston's line of defense, the very same line that Papa and Bud were ordered to join. By the end of February these two important rivers and Nashville, having been given over to General Buell without a fight, were under Union control. Johnston's army was pushed back from Kentucky through Tennessee and concentrated at Corinth, Mississippi, just below the Tennessee border.

On March 17, Grant was given overall command of the Union army in this area, and his 33,000 troops were camped on the Tennessee River at Pittsburgh Landing, just 22 miles northeast of Corinth. Commanding the Army of the Ohio, General Buell had 25,000 troops in Nashville but was on the march to join Grant and then carry out their plan to strike at Johnston. Corinth was an important railroad junction of two major railway lines, especially vital to the Confederacy, and a prize both sides wanted to win.

In order to keep the Yankees from the prize, Johnston knew he must attack Grant before he could be reinforced by Buell. With 45,000 Confederate troops he had to get to Grant before his Rebels were outnumbered. By the end of March Johnston had made his plans. He would move on Pittsburgh Landing and attack Grant there. Surprise would be his best weapon.

And so, the plan was set. On April 3, the Confederate Army of the Mississippi began to move out of Corinth with an attack date for April 5. Somewhere in the line of men Bud was marching. Somewhere on horseback Papa was riding with his men: all going to the same destination, all headed to an unknown fate. The men were confident with General A.S. Johnston as their leader and General P.G.T. Beauregard at his side. And as U.S. Grant was announcing to his subordinate officers on the very afternoon of April 5, "There will be no fighting at Pittsburgh Landing. We will have to go to Corinth," the Rebels were close at hand.

Storms and bad roads delayed the April 5th attack. But on April 6th the sun dawned soft and pink on a peaceful Sunday morning. A light fog covered the ground around a sleepy little church named Shiloh. Around and beyond the church Yankee soldiers lay quiet in their camps, some still sleeping, some stirring about making coffee and frying bacon in their skillets. All looked forward to a day's rest from drilling and training. Sunday meant having leisure time to write letters to loved ones at home, taking a much-needed bath in the river, or just lying around the camp. Little did they know that a massive force of Confederates was quietly moving in, rifles in hand, to destroy them.

It was a beautiful spring day, and Rachel was enjoying the sound of birds and the fresh breeze that was blowing through the open windows of the parlor. She was all alone, and because she had gotten used to having Mama or Suzanna around all the time, she was bored. Usually after church on Sundays Suzanna came home with Rachel and Mama to spend the afternoon, but today, she had not come. Her mother was not doing well, and Suzanna was afraid to leave her alone. Mama had gone to speak to Mr. Gunther about the spring planting. Lily and Lizbet were off doing something in their rooms and couldn't be found. So, Rachel was left to occupy herself for a while, and she was finding it extremely difficult.

Soon she decided to write a letter to Bud. She found several sheets of writing paper, a pen, and a small bottle of ink in Mama's desk. For several minutes, she sat holding the pen and thinking about what to write. She watched a small caterpillar crawl along the window ledge, hummed a few lines of "Praise God From Whom All Blessings Flow" which they had sung in church and was stuck in her head, and played with the ribbon in her hair. There was nothing to write about, and Rachel scowled at the empty page.

Finally, she dipped the pen in the ink bottle and scribbled the date across the top of the letter. Sunday, April 6, 1862. At least now she had begun. Then she wrote, "Dearest Bud." Several more minutes went by as she continued to think about what to write. Nothing important or exciting had happened in so long. She had already written to him about the stray cat in the barn having kittens. He already knew about the cows breaking loose and getting in the bayou. Rachel wished she had funny stories to write about like Bud did. She loved reading his letters.

Rachel put down the pen and stood up; she would finish it later when she could think of something to write about. She walked to the piano and sat down. Because Suzanna enjoyed playing the piano so much Rachel had begun to enjoy it, too. She hated practicing scales and the really hard songs. But, since Mama was not here to correct her fingering and posture, she decided to play a few pieces.

Rachel started with Mozart's "Sonata in C" because she liked the tune, and it wasn't too hard for her, even though there were lots of sixteenth notes running up and down the keyboard. The melody cut through the stillness of the house and echoed from the high walls and ceiling of the parlor. Next, she tried Beethoven's "Fur Elise," Mama's favorite, and Rachel surprised herself at how beautifully she played it.

At that moment Rachel heard a door open. She hesitated for a second and listened. She thought it might be Mama coming home or Lily coming to see about her. But there was no sound. The house was silent. So she began her song again. It must have been her imagination.

Then she heard another noise. It sounded like someone in the hallway. Without stopping her music Rachel glanced over her shoulder to see if someone was there. But again, there was nothing. She frowned to think she might be scaring herself.

She continued to play, but with each note her ears were straining to hear any sound. There it was again. This time she had heard footsteps. The breeze blowing warm through the open windows suddenly turned cool and made the room chilly. A strange tingling ran up Rachel's spine and made her shiver. The tiny hairs on her arms began to bristle, and she got goosebumps. She didn't dare turn around, but from the corner of her eye, she could see the figure of a man standing in the parlor entry. Rachel held her breath as the man drew closer. She could feel his presence rather than see him because she could not bring herself to turn around.

Rachel wanted to scream or call out to anyone for help, but her voice would not work. Even stranger yet was that her fingers would not stop playing. Her music continued to fill the air, and the man stood motionless behind her. He was dressed in gray, and Rachel could see from glancing back over her shoulder that his boots were covered in mud, and his coat was ragged. He did not say a word but seemed to be captivated by the melody.

Rachel couldn't see his face. She was too afraid to turn and get a good look at the stranger. Petrified, she was unable to move any part of her body except her nimble fingers that had never played so well before. Finally, the piece ended, and Rachel played the last note. She took a deep breath, lifted her fingers from the keys, and waited. She expected the man to speak or grab her or shoot her in the back. But nothing happened.

When Rachel finally got the nerve to turn and face him, much to her surprise, he was gone. She was stunned and still too afraid to move from the piano bench. He might be hiding in the hall or in the kitchen. Rachel listened for a long time. Minutes passed that seemed like hours until Rachel again heard someone in the hall. She stiffened and held her breath.

"Rachel, dear, Rachel, are you in here?" It was Mama, and Rachel burst into tears.

"What on earth!" gasped Mama as she ran to her daughter. She caught Rachel just as she was collapsing on the small bench. Mama carried her to the sofa and called for Lily.

Later in the kitchen, Mama, Lily, and Lizbet listened quietly as Rachel told of her experience. The fear on their faces reflected the fear Rachel had felt during that brief visit: Lizbet's eyes widened with each word as Rachel described the stranger; Lily grunted and shook her head while Mama frowned in deep thought.

"You say his boots were muddy?" Mama asked when Rachel had finished.

Rachel nodded.

Mama quickly stood up and left the room. Lily was close on her heels. Lizbet and Rachel stared at each other with puzzled looks. Then, as if they were afraid to be left in the room by themselves, they both jumped up and followed their mothers.

Mama and Lily were standing in the hall, looking down. They were examining the floor when the two girls slipped up behind them. They watched as Mama went into the parlor then to the front door and out onto the porch. No one said a word. No one made eye contact. Everyone was seeing the same thing, or rather, *not* seeing the same thing.

There was not a speck of mud anywhere on the floors. Not a footprint could be seen. The mysterious man with the muddy boots had come and gone without a trace.

"Lawd, bless my soul," whispered Lily. "I done heared such tales b'fo' but Lawsy, I done nevuh see it fo' myse'f."

Lizbet's eyes looked like white saucers. She whispered to Rachel,

"You b'lieve he be *uh... uh you know ghos'*?"

Rachel was shocked. A ghost? It couldn't have been. It was a man, a man in gray. She had seen him with her own eyes.

"Don't be silly," Rachel snapped at Lizbet, turned and went to her room.

Rachel would never know who or what she had seen that April day. It was a subject that no one mentioned or discussed. But it was a day Rachel would never forget. Although she did not know it then, this first Sunday in April would be unforgettable for more reasons than a strange visitor. A bloody battle was raging at the same time a ghost had come to call.

The sun was not yet up when Bud awakened with his men. Some had slept by fires built in holes in the ground to avoid detection by the enemy just across the way. Others had not slept at all, being too anxious about the impending attack. All were hungry as they had eaten their three-day rations the first day. Their joints were stiff from sleeping on the hard ground, and they shivered from the cool, damp air. They moved in silence as they checked rifles and cartridge boxes.

Unaware that their trusted general, Beauregard, had argued with Johnston throughout the night to withdraw back to Corinth, they prepared to form ranks with the same confidence they had shown throughout the march here. Beauregard, on the other hand, was not at all confident. He was convinced that Buell had arrived from Nashville, and there were now 70,000 troops facing them. He was also certain they had lost the element of surprise and were headed for disaster.

General Johnston, however, stood firm. He would not hear of withdrawing, not now, not after the long, hard march from Corinth to bring the fight to the Federals. "I would fight them if they were a million," he told a member of his staff. So the die was cast. There was no turning back.

Bud wiped sweat from his brow, not from heat, for it was cool standing in the dark. His hands were cold and clammy as he waited beside his men for the signal to advance. He looked up at the sky. Stars in the east were fading as the sun, not yet visible, was lighting the sky. The western sky was still dotted with twinkling stars. It reminded Bud of pre-dawn hunting trips he had made with Papa. He gripped his pistol. This was a strange hunting trip, hunting men instead of game, being hunted as well.

Papa was here, somewhere, but Bud hadn't seen him in several weeks. The cavalry had been on the move, scouting and gathering information, as the army had prepared to march. There were reports that ten cavalrymen had been captured the night before and were being held as prisoners. Bud hoped that Papa was not one of them nor Evan Millbrook, a new father now, who had also joined the cavalry. He hated to think what might happen to either of them in the enemy camp.

Bud's mouth was dry, and he tried to swallow. He wanted to drink from his canteen, but he had already ordered his small group of men to conserve their water for the long day ahead. Bud thought about his men; most were boys really, among them his longtime friend, Tom Harrison, and two of his brothers who were old enough to enlist, Joseph and Adam. His other childhood friend, Robert Yancey, was somewhere on the line also serving as second lieutenant. They were all part of the 6th Mississippi and eager for their first battle. The waiting had been the worst part—nervous stomachs, pacing, praying—but now there was an eerie calm over the silent group.

Finally, word came down to advance. The mass of men in gray began to rumble across the open fields. Flocks of birds rustled from the trees and lifted high in the air as they were disturbed from their quiet roosts. Small rabbits, squirrels, and foxes were shaken out of their burrows and scampered away out of the path of the oncoming bulk of men. There was a heavy morning mist on the ground making the soldiers look ghostly as they made their way toward the enemy.

At 5:14 a.m. the first shots were fired. The picket guards were easily swept away as they ran to warn their commanders. If the Rebels' approach had indeed been a sur-

prise it was a surprise no longer. The alarm was quickly sounded. "Rebels comin'!" got every Yankee soldier on his feet.

Bud's heart pounded as the first white Union tents came into view. They were camped around the Methodist church called Shiloh Chapel, and Bud saw the regimental flag of the 53rd Ohio. He knew this to be part of General William Tecumseh Sherman's division, his former professor and old friend. Bud knew that Sherman was under the command of General Grant, but it had not occurred to him that they would actually be facing each other on the battlefield. This was not the kind of reunion he wanted to have.

Suddenly, popping sounds broke their silent approach. The Yankees were firing at them. The Rebels only quickened their pace as they plunged into the Yankee camps. Everything began to happen at once. Many of Sherman's men dropped their guns, skillets, or pants and ran to the banks of the Tennessee. But, many more held their ground on a ridge where their tents were pitched, firing at the wave of gray soldiers coming across the valley at them.

Bud urged his men onward. Some stopped to take aim and fire. Others stopped to reload, but the line continued to roll forward. They pushed as far as they could go up the slope of the ridge, but the firing was so heavy, they had to fall back into the woods. Smoke from so many guns and dust stirred up from so many feet grew thick in the air, making it hard to breathe. The Rebels fell against trees or on the ground, heaving and panting and trying to catch their breaths. They were all relieved they had escaped the flying bullets.

Bud looked back over the ground they had just covered. He was horrified at the sight. Dead and wounded bodies of his comrades lay strewn across the field, their time in the war and on earth cut too short. It was a sight that would unnerve the bravest heart had there been time to think on it, but, as soon as the men had taken to the woods, they were ordered to charge again.

This time the Rebels rushed into the open with their high-pitched, blood-curdling yell, the sound that sent shivers up even the strongest Yankee spine. The line of gray ran toward the slope again. Almost immediately, the Yankee rifles exploded in a blaze of bullets. There were screams and curses, men falling and men yelling, agonizing cries mixed with angry shouts. The Rebels pulled back again to safety from the unmerciful Federal bullets, leaving more dead and wounded in their wake.

The five Confederate regiments in this assault were determined to push back the Yankees to the Tennessee River, and they charged the slope three more times. On the fifth and final attempt, the Yankees could hold no longer and retreated as the Mississippi boys took over their camp. Cheers rang out from the Rebel force as they stood on the ridge and stared at the bountiful goods the Yanks had left behind. There was meat still frying in skillets, coffee still warm in pots, shoes, guns, water canteens. Hungry soldiers snatched up their breakfast and rummaged through the tents.

The officers tried to restore order as best they could. Bud was calling for his men through the smoke, dust, and confusion. He looked back onto the field over which they had just passed, and the sight was sickening. Bodies lay thick on the ground, some wounded and writhing in pain, missing arms or legs and stumbling around in shock, but most were dead: their eyes still open and their hands still clutching their rifles. Bud thought of all the women who would soon learn about their loved ones and weep for their losses. He laid his hand on his breast pocket where he kept the two ribbons, one blue, one yellow, close to his heart.

But, there was no time for mourning the dead or remembering loved ones. The men must regroup and resume the attack. Bud looked for the flag bearer. He saw a young soldier sitting on a rock with the flag draped across his lap. It was the very same flag sewn by Mama and the other ladies and presented to his company by his dear Suzanna. Bud had seen the colors go down at least three times during the attacks, and someone had always swept the flag up and continued on.

When Bud got near to the boy, he saw that the youth was sobbing uncontrollably. His whole body was trembling, and Bud put his hand on the boy's shoulder to steady him. The young soldier looked up at Bud with red, fearful eyes. His face was streaked by tears that ran down his sooty face. Bud now recognized the boy whose name was Jimmy.

"It ain't what I thought it'd be," he muttered and looked over his shoulder at the field below. "It ain't what I thought at all."

"Me either," said Bud. Even though Bud and Jimmy were close in age, Bud seemed much older. "You did fine. Real fine. Now let's finish it."

The young Rebel studied Bud's face. He searched Bud's blue eyes for reassurance or deliverance or, maybe, just a bit of courage. Finally, he nodded, smiled, and wiped his dirty face with an equally dirty hand. Then he stood up and waved the flag so the men in Bud's company could find them. They soon discovered that the dash across the valley to take the ridge on which they now stood had been more than treacherous. It had been devastating. Of the 425 men in the whole 6th Mississippi only about a hundred had made it still standing. It was just the beginning of a long, bloody day.

As the Confederates were wasting time filling their stomachs and pockets, Sherman's men had taken up a new position and were making ready for another Rebel attack. Other divisions had been brought up to form a strong line extending from the Tennessee River to the western border of the Federal camp. The Yankees were ready to defend and were just as determined not to be pushed into the river as the Confederates were determined to do it. Only one division of Buell's army had arrived at Pittsburgh Landing as yet, so contrary to Beauregard's fears, the numbers of both sides were just about equal. It would be a hard struggle between two brave armies.

The Rebel force was hastily reorganized. Bud was put in command of a new company made up of survivors from the 6th and placed under the immediate command of General Braxton Bragg. The advance continued toward the center of the Union defense where a division under the command of General Prentiss had established a strong position in a sunken wagon trail. The sunken road was bordered by an open field to its front and heavy woods to its back. As they had done earlier that morning, the Rebels gave their yell and charged across the field toward the muzzles of Federal rifles.

Now high in the sky, the sun added to the heat that was on the ground. Bud wiped sweat mixed with gunpowder and dirt from his eyes. The charge that had just been made was repulsed, and the men were waiting in the safety of the trees for further orders. Soldiers were coughing, choking from the smoke and heat. They lay against the trunks of trees and heaved noisily as they tried to catch their breaths. Water was in great demand. Canteens were passed around until the last drop was gone. Before the men had time to think, the order to charge again was given. Bud joined the other weary soldiers as they lifted rifles and headed across the field. Again the firing was too heavy to advance further, and a retreat was necessary. Each time the wave of gray receded to the woods it left more dead and wounded in its wake. Bud wondered how many times it would take before they were all lying on the field.

The struggle to push back the Yankees from the sunken road became so fierce that it quickly became known as the 'Hornets' Nest.' Time after time the Rebels charged, but Prentiss and his men stood firm. To the right of the Hornets' Nest another attack was being made on Union General Hurlburt whose men were posted among the trees of a ten-acre peach orchard. It was later recalled by the fighting men that the gunfire was so heavy peach blossoms shot from the trees filled the sky and rained down like a heavenly snowfall.

All up and down the line fighting was continuous. The boom of the cannon and crack of the rifles were relentless and constant. General Johnston rode his horse along the line speaking to the men: boosting morale and inspiring courage. The sight of him did give the weak-hearted a new strength and the bone-tired a new burst of energy. But it proved deadly for the general.

As he rejoiced with his men on successfully pushing Hurlburt from the peach orchard, a minie ball struck him in the leg right above the knee. Because he had sent his surgeon to care for a group of wounded Federal prisoners, there was no one who could help stop the bleeding. In only a short time General Albert Sidney Johnston was dead.

By now it was 2:30 in the afternoon. The struggle for the Hornets' Nest was still going on. Word had not reached the fighting men that their commander-in-chief was dead. Orders demanded that they not know until the battle was over. Such news might slash morale in already weary soldiers and turn the tide in favor of the Yankees.

The heat and smoke were unbearable. Bud's chest heaved as he lay under a big oak. His mouth and throat were so dry he couldn't speak. How many times had they run across the field only to be sent reeling back? He had lost count.

Bud looked at the men around him. The day had taken its toll. They lay like rag dolls on the ground and against the trees, arms and legs so tired that they hung limp and lifeless. Clothes were torn from running through brambles, and a layer of dust covered each man from head to toe, making them all look strangely gray. But, it was the faces that had changed over the long hours of battle. Wide eyes stared blankly from expressionless faces. All emotion seemed to have been drained and replaced with shock. Men moved and spoke as if in a dream, or rather, a nightmare, from which they couldn't wake up.

When the order rang out once more to form ranks and renew the charge, an old man with a stubby, gray-speckled beard called out in an exhausted voice,

"Let's git 'em this time, boys. We been at this here game long enough."

A wild-eyed teenaged boy let out the Rebel yell, and an electrifying wave went through the whole line of attackers. A mysterious power swept through each man that overcame the exhaustion and fear. In one great rush the Rebels were comin' again.

Bud had almost gotten used to the whiz of bullets past his head, the sight of a fellow soldier being blown off his feet, and the screams of the wounded. He ran without looking or thinking, his eyes and mind concentrating on the objective ahead. Close by, just ahead in the midst of the men and dust, Bud could see young Jimmy running with the colors held high. And just as Bud focused on the flag, he saw it suddenly fall. At that moment all Bud could think was to get to the boy. He was almost trampled on by his own men, but somehow he managed to make it to the spot where the boy and the flag had gone down.

There lay Jimmy, clutching his side and wailing in pain. Bud quickly pulled back Jimmy's hand and revealed a large, dark red stain on his shirt. Jimmy looked up at Bud with terror on his face.

"You're gonna be fine," Bud tried to reassure the frightened boy. "We'll get help. Just lie still."

Just then, a big, burly soldier with thick hands ran to the flag and snatched it up. In one swift motion he raised the staff high and was gone with the tide of men rolling by.

Bud gathered up the wounded Jimmy in his arms and stood up. The boy lay limp and quiet. Just then, Bud felt a sharp pain in his arm. He stumbled backward from the force and almost dropped his burden. His arm was on fire, and he checked to see if the limb was still there.

It was, but his sleeve above the elbow was dark red, and blood was running down his hand. He dropped to his

155

knees, being too weak to hold Jimmy and stand upright. He gently laid the boy back on the ground. The earth was spinning. Bud could no longer see clearly, everything was a blur. His ears were ringing. Then everything went black.

10
When Angels Weep

april 7, 1862

NEWS OF THE BATTLE OF SHILOH didn't reach Mama and Rachel until the next day, Monday afternoon. On Sunday night church bells had rung in Jackson in celebration of a southern victory. People puffed out their chests like proud roosters and laughed when they heard Beauregard had slept that night in Sherman's tent. The Federals had been pushed back, not into the river as hoped or even away from Pittsburgh Landing, but they had given up enough ground to warrant a Confederate win.

Suzanna's buggy came flying down the lane with Uncle Phillip as driver. She jumped from her seat without waiting for her uncle's hand and ran into the house. Although a spring rain was coming down she was bareheaded with no umbrella and, therefore, wet from head to toe. Mama quickly called Lily to bring a towel, but before anyone could get Suzanna dry or calmed down, she spilled out the news as fast as she could talk.

"There's been a fight!" she exclaimed in a frantic voice.

Mama's knees went weak, and she almost swooned. But Uncle Phillip steadied her as Suzanna carried on without taking a breath.

"Bud's been in a fight," she said. "The troops in Corinth moved into Tennessee, south of Savannah, where Grant's troops were camped. There was a battle, a terrible one, and we pushed the Yankees back. We won…"

Rachel let out a cry of joy, but Suzanna and Mama hushed her quickly. Rachel looked confused and hurt.

"It's good news that we won" Suzanna assured Rachel. "But, oh, hon', it was at such an awful price."

Then Suzanna began to sob, and Mama wrapped her arms around her.

Clinging to each other, they moved into the parlor and sat down. Suzanna was sobbing uncontrollably now.

Rachel felt a strange tingle all over her body. She remembered the strange visitor, the 'ghost' according to Lizbet, who had come to call on the very afternoon of the battle. It was an ominous sign, and it made her shudder. Rachel turned to Suzanna's uncle, and with tears in her eyes she asked softly, "Has something happened to Bud?"

Uncle Phillip squatted down to Rachel's level and, wiping a tear from her cheek, said, "We don't know, dear. There's been no news of Bud or your father. All we know

is that there were many casualties; many men have been killed or wounded."

Then Rachel began to sob. The room was heavy with anxiety and gloom. Outside, the rain came down faster and harder, seemingly trying to outdo the flood of tears that were flowing inside the house. Poor Uncle Phillip didn't know what to do to comfort the distraught women, so he just stood nearby wringing his hands. And the three women would've cried themselves sick if it hadn't been for Mama.

She suddenly stood up, wiped her eyes and face with her handkerchief, and pulled back her shoulders. She spoke with an unusual calmness.

"Now, we'll just have to stop this nonsense," she demanded. "We don't know what has happened. For all we know, our men are sitting in their tents right now writing to us about the glorious battle. We'll just have to have faith. It does no one any good to sit and weep away the hours."

Mama had spoken, and when Mama spoke with such authority, she was obeyed. All tears ceased. Suzanna dabbed at her red eyes, and Rachel snubbed and sniffled until her chest finally stopped heaving. Surely this was what Mama meant when, months ago, she had said that they must be brave. Rachel felt it was harder to sit at home and not know what was happening than to actually be on the battlefield. The waiting was unbearable.

Mr. Yancey, their closest neighbor and Robert's father, came late on Monday night with the shocking

news about the fallen General Johnston. By now, the whole Confederacy, fighting men as well, knew of his death, and everyone felt saddened and fearful over the loss of a great leader. There was word that the battle had resumed at dawn this morning, but the details were as yet unknown. Another wire he had received just a few hours earlier confirmed their worst fears. General Buell had arrived on the scene sometime late Sunday night to reinforce the Yankees. The Rebels had awakened to face a stronger, fresher force than the previous day. The tables had turned. All Mr. Yancey could tell Mama, Suzanna, and Rachel was that Beauregard and his men were heading back to Corinth. He had no word from his son or anyone else who had been on the battlefield.

The news could have started a deluge of tears again, but Mama sat still and rigid. Her face was pale, eerily pale, and she thanked Mr. Yancey with a quiet, solemn voice. There was nothing to do but wait.

The church bells did not ring on Monday night in Jackson. Everyone felt defeat. A great Confederate general was dead, Grant was still encamped in Tennessee, having taken back all the ground lost on the first day of fighting, and the Army of the Mississippi was back where they started, except that they had left many brave men behind. It was no time to celebrate.

Each day without a word from Bud or Papa became more and more unbearable for the Franklin women. Casualty lists had not yet been compiled and posted, and no one seemed to know their whereabouts. Rachel wished they could just jump in the buggy, go to the army, and find out for themselves. Mama tried to keep all of them busy so that they wouldn't pace the floor or sit and wring their hands or, worst yet, burst into tears. But, the waiting was exhausting.

Then, finally, the waiting was over.

It happened on Thursday. Mama had taken Suzanna and Rachel to the garden to help plant the spring vegetables. All three of them were bent low over the rich soil, big hat brims flopping in the wind as they dropped tiny seeds and carefully covered them with soft dirt. Lily and Lizbet were toiling over the laundry on the other side of the house when they spied a wagon rolling down the lane toward the house. Lily straightened up and squinted against the bright morning sun. She stared for several minutes trying to make out who the visitors were. Then her eyes got big, and she began to whoop in a high-pitched voice. She dropped a large bedsheet on the ground and took off at break-neck speed.

"Miz Belle! Miz Belle!" she screamed. "Dey's comin'! Dey's comin'!"

Mama straightened up, holding down her hat on her head with one hand, and watched Lily curiously. When Lily finally reached the garden she was totally out of breath and couldn't speak.

"What on earth?" Mama exclaimed. "What are you yellin' about, Lily?"

"Dey's... dey's..." Lily wheezed and panted. "Dey's comin'."

"Who's coming? Lily, what are you talking about?" Mama headed toward Lily to see if she had a fever.

Lily took one big breath and blurted out. "Missuh William he comin' and he got Missuh Bud's hoss tie' to de wagon."

"Oh, my Lord!" Mama called out and, dropping her basket of seeds, took off running with Rachel and Suzanna right behind her.

When they reached the front of the house, Papa was pulling the wagon up to the front steps. He quickly tied down the reins and jumped off the seat. He did not rush to the women, but, rather, he ran to the back of the wagon and began pulling something out. The women ran to help him, and when they saw what it was, they gasped at the same time.

It was Bud. His eyes were closed, and he was as limp as a rag doll.

Thinking he was dead, Suzanna screamed and fell in a heap on the ground.

"He's all right. He's alive," Papa grunted as he strained to lift Bud from the buckboard. He managed to get his arms under Bud's tall body and carry him like a little child. Mama ran ahead and opened the door. Rachel stayed with Suzanna, urging her to get up and go in the house to see about Bud.

Papa laid Bud on the sofa in the parlor. Mama was calling Lily to bring all manner of things: hot water, bandages, a blanket, towels, and food. Rachel and Suzanna stood back and stared at Bud's lifeless body. They hardly

recognized him. He was covered in dirt and dried blood. His black hair was nearly gray from the dust. His face was black from gunpowder, and his arm was wrapped in a dirty, bloody bandage from shoulder to wrist.

Suzanna could stand it no longer. She rushed to Bud's side and fell on her knees, pressing her face on his chest. She sobbed and caressed his blackened face until Mama came with a pan of warm water and a towel. Only then did she move away and let Mama gently wash her son's face. Papa put his arm around Suzanna's shoulder and led her over to a chair.

"He's been shot in the arm," Papa explained. "He's lost a lot of blood."

Just then, the front door flew open, and in rushed Dr. Prentiss. Close on his heels, of course, was Miss Rosalee. Everyone but Papa looked up in surprise.

"I sent a message ahead for the doctor to meet us here," he said softly. Then he addressed Dr. Prentiss.

"Please come in, Sam. We've just gotten here ourselves. We've been on the road for two days. The trip was hard on Bud. I'm afraid he's lost a lot of blood."

Dr. Prentiss charged across the room, carrying his black bag, and with an air of complete authority, waved everyone away. Mama took her time and finished wiping the last smudge from Bud's face. Then she calmly moved to the end of the sofa and sat at Bud's feet. She was determined to stay close to her son.

The doctor first listened to Bud's heart. Satisfied that he was still alive, he then began to unwrap the filthy ban-

dage. Bud moved and groaned when Dr. Prentiss lifted his injured arm and let it slip out of his hands and drop on the sofa.

"Please, Sam," Mama pleaded.

Dr. Prentiss peered over his glasses at all the females in the room.

"It might be a good idea if the ladies go into another room," he said. "This could be a rather gory sight."

Mama wasn't budging, nor would Suzanna leave her husband's side. Miss Rosalee wouldn't dream of being left out. Why, the re-telling of this day could keep her the center of attention for many sewing groups and church socials to come. Rachel sat quietly and watched Papa, waiting for him to point the way out, but, to her surprise, he didn't. His eyes were glued to Bud.

Dr. Prentiss realized no one intended to obey him, so with a little snort of agitation, he turned his attention back to his patient. With each twist of the bloody cloth Bud moaned and tossed. Suzanna jumped up from her seat across the room and rushed to the end of the sofa where Bud's head lay. She put her dainty hands on his forehead and caressed his hair. Bud opened his eyes for only a brief moment, but everyone was sure Bud had recognized his bride and knew he was home.

Rachel stared at the long strip of bandage as it fell in folds on the floor. She watched as it turned from dirty white to dark red to black. A wave of nausea surged through her body. She wanted to run out of the room and hide, but something was compelling her to sit frozen in

her chair. She wanted to look away, but her eyes stayed focused on the scene before her. She wanted to press her hands tightly against her ears so she couldn't hear Bud's cries of pain, but no part of her body would move.

Dr. Prentiss bent low over Bud's arm as the last of the bandage fell to the floor. Suzanna gasped and buried her face in Bud's dirty hair. The wound was a large, black hole right above the elbow, caked with dried blood and dirt. The doctor studied it for a long time, then he began to probe. This made Bud writhe on the narrow sofa and cry out in pain.

"Don't take my arm!" he yelled out. "Don't do it!"

Bud began to rant about cutting off his arm as he bucked like a wild bronco, struggling to free himself from Dr. Prentiss's grip. Papa quickly moved to help the doctor. He held Bud down, firmly but gently, and assured him repeatedly that he would keep his arm. Suzanna was still holding his head as he slung back and forth, talking softly in his ear to calm his fears. Mama sat as rigid as a wooden doll at Bud's feet while Miss Rosalee sat across the room, sniffling and wiping her eyes.

All their efforts worked, or else, Bud was just too weak to struggle longer for he suddenly went limp again and lay unconscious. Suzanna whimpered and kissed his forehead for the hundredth time. Papa relaxed his grip and straightened up. He stepped back and knelt beside Mama, hugging her around the waist. She wrapped her arm around his shoulder. Only then did Rachel get a good look at Bud's wound. The movement had reopened the

gaping hole, and dark blood was oozing from it and dripping on the floor.

Rachel felt her stomach turn. Everything inside her suddenly came to her throat, and there was a bitter taste in her mouth. She knew she was going to be sick and didn't want to make a scene. So she jumped up and ran to the front door. She barely made it to the edge of the porch when her body began to wretch violently. Then she fell on her knees, coughing and spitting. As she tried to catch her breath, a hand touched her shoulder.

"You aw'right?"

It was Lizbet.

Rachel turned and sank down on the porch, resting her back against the house. Lizbet offered the corner of her apron. Rachel wiped her mouth on it and took a deep breath.

"I'm fine," she answered, disgusted at herself that she had not been stronger in a time of crisis.

Lizbet sat down beside Rachel. They listened to the voices just inside the house. Dr. Prentiss was getting flustered with the situation, fuming that the ball was too deep, the bone may be broken but it was too difficult to tell, and, blast it, there was just not enough room to work here on this sofa. They heard Bud cry out as an attempt was made to move him from the sofa to his bed upstairs. Lizbet grabbed onto Rachel's arm and squeezed each time they heard the screams.

When nothing more could be heard but a few muffled voices and dull thuds, Lizbet spoke up.

"Missuh Bud, he hurt real bad."

Rachel nodded.

"Mama say dey might hab' to cut off his arm," she added.

"No!" Rachel snapped back. "No, Papa promised. They have to get the bullet out, that's all. And then… and then he'll be all right."

Time seemed to stop as the two girls sat waiting. Soon a voice could be heard calling for Lizbet. It was Lily, no doubt needing her to do some chore. Lizbet jumped up and took off, leaving Rachel to pass the hours by herself.

It was peaceful there on the porch. A nice, spring breeze was blowing. Occasionally, a bird would chirp. Somewhere in the distance a rooster was crowing. So different from the world inside the house. A world of pain and suffering, worry and fear. Rachel thought about how quickly everything had turned upside down. Not only her family and their lives, but the whole world. Everything had changed, and she wondered if things would ever be the same again.

The afternoon sun moved slowly across the sky, and still Rachel sat on the porch. She was afraid to go back into the house. She didn't want to hear the screams anymore. She didn't want to see another drop of blood. She couldn't look at her father's face, his darkened, wide eyes and sunken cheeks. He looked as if he had not slept or eaten for days.

Finally, the front door opened. Rachel looked up to see Miss Rosalee standing over her.

"Your mother wants you, dear," she said in a surprisingly soft voice.

Rachel stood up, and much to her own surprise, she wrapped her arms around Miss Rosalee's large, round waist and buried her face in her dress. She began to weep while Miss Rosalee stroked her hair.

"It's all right, hon'," she said soothingly. "Everything's going to be all right. Dr. Prentiss removed the bullet, and Bud's going to be just fine. Why, with all the good nursing he'll get around here, he'll be on his feet in no time."

Miss Rosalee patted Rachel gently on the back and led her into the house. Rachel tried not to look into the parlor, but from the corner of her eye, she could see Lily on her hands and knees beside the sofa. Rachel knew she was cleaning up the horrible mess that would be forever etched in the family's minds. Miss Rosalee walked Rachel into the dining room where Papa and Mama were seated.

By now, it was late in the afternoon, almost dark, and dark shadows fell across the room. Papa motioned for Rachel to come to him. He picked her up and sat her on his lap. She laid her head on his chest while he stroked her soft curls. They were all exhausted, and no one spoke. The silence was finally broken when Dr. Prentiss entered the room. He was breathing heavily as he turned down the sleeves of his blood-stained shirt. Miss Rosalee buttoned the cuffs for him and wiped his forehead.

"Well, William... Belle... I've done all I can do," the doctor said seriously. "He's in the good Lord's hands now... and yours." He nodded toward Mama. "He's going to

need some powerful good nursin'. And I know he'll get it."

The doctor and his wife moved wearily to the door. Dr. Prentiss stopped and turned,

"He's weak, very weak right now," he shook his head. "But I know your son, known him since he was born, and he's a strong one. I think he'll be fine... just fine."

Papa thanked the doctor again. Promising to check on Bud in a few days, Dr. Prentiss and Miss Rosalee left. The room was silent once more.

After a long while Jo and Mott came in and lit the lamps. A few minutes later they appeared again with warm food for dinner. No one really felt like eating, but it had been a long day without food. They knew they needed to eat something. Suzanna had not left Bud's bedside throughout the whole ordeal, and Mama asked Mott to take a tray to her.

The whole day had been more than a brain or a heart could handle, and talking about it was out of the question. So, the small family picked at their food in silence, each one thinking, or rather trying not to think, about everything that had taken place.

Finally, Papa broke the silence.

"It was a miracle that I found Bud," he began. "There was so much confusion, so much noise, so much gunfire... smoke so thick, you could hardly breathe or see which direction to go... so many men, wounded and dying." Papa stopped and looked at Mama and Rachel, as if he

had forgotten they were in the room. He dropped his head for a moment, then began again,

"I got word about mid-afternoon that Bud's company was engaged in trying to push back General Prentiss… no relation to our dear doctor I presume," Papa managed a smile that quickly faded. "The Yankees were entrenched in a sunken road, and it was like running headlong into a wall of bullets. Men returning from the charges were calling it the 'Hornets' Nest.'"

Rachel knew the fierceness of hornets and how hotly they could sting. The thought of bullets instead of hornets was horrifying. She looked at Mama who sat motionless. Her green eyes stared blankly at Papa as he continued his story.

"My men were dismounted and pressing a charge on the right of Bud's unit, trying to push back Hurlburt's division." Papa raised up in his chair and leaned toward Mama. "Somewhere in between the Union divisions of Prentiss and Hurlburt was Sherman's division."

Finally, Mama reacted. The name of their friend, William T. Sherman, caused her to sigh heavily, press her fingers to her forehead, and shake her head. It was all so awful it was hard to absorb.

"We made no less than seven attacks," Papa continued. "We pushed them back from a peach orchard, a sight I will never forget. The bullets cut into the blossoms so furiously that they came down like so many snowflakes."

Rachel tried to picture this in her mind. What a

beautiful sight that would be had it not been for the cause of it.

"The fighting seemed to go on without stopping," Papa said. "The heat… the thirst… the carnage… it was almost unbearable."

Papa stopped to catch his breath. He squeezed the bridge of his nose as if trying to pinch back tears. Perhaps he was remembering too clearly, and the *re-living* was more than he could stand. Mama and Rachel waited quietly as Papa composed himself.

"It was late in the day, around four o'clock I think, but I can't be sure," Papa frowned as he spoke. "Hurlburt's men finally retreated, leaving Prentiss still anchored on the sunken road. When the division on his right gave way as well, Prentiss found himself surrounded. After eleven maybe twelve hours of hard fighting, Prentiss surrendered."

Papa acted more like a man who had suffered defeat in the battle rather than victory. There was no joy over the surrender of the enemy, no signs of pride in their retreat.

"It was not yet dark when I finally organized my men and secured the prisoners," Papa sighed. "It was then that I went looking for Bud. I reached the field in front of the Hornets' nest and the sight… the sight," Papa now broke down. He sobbed into his hands.

Mama quickly came to his side, wrapped her arms around him, and cried with him. Rachel had never seen her father cry before, and it was almost too much for her. She threw herself on his lap, and the three of them wept together.

"The men lay so thick on the ground there was hardly room to walk between them," Papa sobbed again. "There seemed no hope of finding Bud. I didn't know where to turn… but somehow I *did* find him, and thank the Lord, it wasn't on that field. He had been taken to a makeshift hospital… and it… it was too horrible to describe."

Papa took out his handkerchief and wiped his face again. He looked into Mama's face and caressed her hair. She knew how painful it was for him to tell this story.

"If I hadn't gotten there when I did, our son wouldn't have his arm," Papa said. "The surgeons were taking limbs… arms… legs… as fast as they could take a saw to them."

Both Mama and Rachel cringed and shuddered to think of it. Under normal circumstances Papa would never have mentioned such terrible things in front of them, but he needed them to understand what was going on. The war was no longer something that happened someplace faraway. The war had come home. It was happening to the Franklins, and no one would be spared.

"Bud and I spent the night in a tent, a Federal tent," Papa managed another quick smile. "There was a terrible rainstorm, but, thank goodness, the Yanks make a sturdier tent than we do. Bud tossed feverishly through the night. I managed to get a doctor to see about him, but all that could be done was bandage the wound and cool the fever. Next morning we awoke to find that Grant had been reinforced with fresh troops and was ready to attack. They came on strong, and frankly our boys were all fought out. Beauregard called for retreat around 2:00 that afternoon, and we moved out. The troops headed back to Corinth, but I managed to secure a wagon, and Bud and I headed home."

For a few minutes, all was silent, except for Rachel's sniffling. Then, for the first time since Bud had been laid on the sofa, Rachel heard her mother's voice.

"What about the others, William?" she asked in a quivering voice. "What about Evan and Robert and the Harrison boys? Are they all right?"

Papa did not answer right away, and his hesitation filled Mama and Rachel with dread. They needed to know, but they didn't want to know if the truth was too awful.

"Of course, Evan and I were together. . . in the peach orchard," Papa began. "He... he..."

Mama looked at Papa with pleading eyes. In her heart she was begging to hear that Evan was all right.

"He was hit," Papa managed to say the words. "He was wounded in the leg. All I know is that he made it off the battlefield. In the confusion of trying to find Bud, I don't know what happened to him. Belle, there were so many wounded... so much..."

Mama interrupted, "I know, William. I understand. Let's just pray he made it home. Poor Laura and the baby... let's just pray he made it home."

"And the others," Papa continued. "I have no news of the others. Bud may know when he's able to talk. Robert and the Harrisons were on his line, in front of the Hor-

nets' Nest." Papa shook his head and raised his hand to his face again. Rachel thought he was going to break down a second time and could feel her own tears welling up once more.

Papa pulled Mama tightly against his chest and kissed her cheek. Then he bent over to where Rachel's head lay in his lap and kissed her on the top of the head.

"Our Bud is home, and that's what matters most right now," he said. "Take good care of him for me. I have to get back to Corinth first thing in the morning."

This was a scene that had been repeated too many times over the past year. Each time Papa left for war the good-byes got harder to say; the pain grew deeper, not knowing if he would return. But on the surface there were fewer tears. Mama and Rachel had learned how to straighten their backbones and lift their chins to hide the fear they felt inside. If they didn't harden against the despair they would surely collapse under the weight of it.

By Saturday Bud was finally sitting up. Rachel watched as Suzanna fed him warm broth, spoonful by spoonful. Somehow Bud's filthy, torn uniform had been exchanged for a white, clean nightshirt. His hair had been brushed free of as much dust as possible, but it was clear he needed one good scrubbing to get him back to the old Bud. If he *could* get back to the old Bud.

As Rachel watched her brother she knew there was something different about him, very different. It was his eyes. They were still the same dark blue, still handsome as he looked lovingly at his wife. But the spark, the flash of daring or mischief or zest for life, whatever it was, had been snuffed out. Bud looked more than exhausted. He looked numb and lifeless. And he was especially quiet. He had not yet said a word about the past week. This was not at all the dashing soldier who could talk for hours on end about his adventures. Give him time was what Mama had said, just give him time.

Mama and Lily changed Bud's bandages each day and cleaned the wound. Lily had obtained some kind of ointment made from herbs and extracts and Lord-knows-what-else which she applied directly on the open wound. She claimed she got it from the 'conjure' woman, the old slave with the coal-black eyes whom Rachel had seen on the day of the adventure to the Gunthers. The gooey salve had a sickening smell, and Rachel had to hold her nose and run downstairs whenever Lily brought it out. But, the mysterious medicine apparently worked, for when Dr. Prentiss came the following week, he marveled at Bud's progress.

"Splendid! Splendid!" the doctor remarked as he examined the wound. "Better than I expected... much better. I commend you ladies for a job well done."

Then he replaced the bandage and made a sling for Bud's arm out of a long piece of cloth. He muttered some instructions to Suzanna which Rachel could not hear; then he packed his doctor's bag and motioned Mama to step out into the hallway. Rachel knew better than to follow her mother, but she did stand just inside Bud's door within good listening range.

"Belle, the wound really does look good," Dr. Prentiss stated again. "He'll be healed in no time." Then the doctor hesitated, "But… but I'm worried about his well-being. How are his spirits?"

Mama sighed. "He hasn't said much, except to tell all of us how much he loves us. He's still in a lot of pain, and I suppose, it's difficult to talk about anything."

"Yes, yes," Dr. Prentiss agreed, patting Mama on the shoulder. "He's been through a tragic ordeal. But, he'll come around. Time heals the soul as well as the body."

Dr. Prentiss hesitated again. He was ready to leave, but Rachel could tell that he still had something on his mind.

"Uh I don't suppose you've heard any news about the battle, that is," he continued.

Mama calmly answered 'no' but her body tensed, and her hands began to shake.

"It's not good," the doctor lamented. "The Yancey boy was killed. The family's taking it hard. Their only consolation is that they were able to get his body and bring it home. He's buried in their oak grove. I'm sorry to have to tell you this, Belle, but I thought you'd want to know."

"Yes, yes, Sam," Mama answered. "Oh, poor dear Camille and John. They've lost their son, their only son."

Rachel could hear Mama sob quietly as she asked, "And what about Tom Harrison… and his brother, Joseph… and the youngest one… Adam, I think his name is. Do you have news of them?"

Dr. Prentiss shook his head and heaved audibly.

"Joe's missing, probably taken prisoner," he sighed. "And as for Tom... frankly I don't know. His name didn't appear on the casualty list just recently posted. We can only hope he's safely back in Corinth with the rest of the survivors. But the younger brother, Adam, only sixteen, was killed."

Mama drew in a quick breath in response to the sad news.

"And Evan Millbrook," Mama said almost in a whisper. "William said he was hit. Do you have any news of Evan?"

Dr. Prentiss nodded and took Mama by the elbow.

"He's lost a leg."

Mama quickly covered her mouth with her hand to stifle a cry. She grabbed the stairpost with the other hand while the doctor steadied her around the waist. From Rachel's position of eavesdropping she heard the shocking news and almost cried out herself. She didn't want to arouse Suzanna or Bud's attention, so she had to keep herself perfectly still and straight-faced until she could escape to her own room and bawl.

"Oh, poor Evan," Mama gasped. "How dreadfully awful for all of them."

Mama and Dr. Prentiss moved slowly down the stairs as the doctor continued to speak,

"I don't know how much Bud knows. I think it best not to say too much until he's more stable. The trauma's been too much for him already."

179

The voices faded out as Mama walked Dr. Prentiss to the front door. Neither Suzanna nor Bud heard any of their conversation as Bud was feeling a lot of pain from the examination, and Suzanna was busy trying to soothe him. Neither one was paying any attention to Rachel as she hurried out of their room and into her own.

So much was spinning in her mind. Her face was hot, and her eyes burned with tears. She thought of tall, handsome Evan Millbrook and beautiful Miss Laura and the baby she had never seen. How could such a horrible thing happen? And Robert Yancey. Dead. Rachel could hardly believe it. She remembered his face, young, energetic, laughing, as Bud and he galloped recklessly on their horses, always getting into as much mischief as they could. And now, Bud lay on his bed, shocked and blank-eyed while his good friend lay buried in the cold, dark ground. Rachel cried. She cried hard and wondered if she would ever stop crying for the rest of her life.

Day after day Suzanna and Rachel sat by Bud's bed and talked of ordinary things. They tried to play the games they had enjoyed so much at Christmas. They brought him his favorite foods. They sang to him and read to him. But no matter what they did, Bud would not be shaken from his melancholia. His arm was healing quickly, but his spirit was still wounded.

The nights were even worse. Bud woke up every night, tossing and screaming, calling out names no one recognized, waking in a terrible sweat. Suzanna did her best to comfort and assure him, but she was close to exhaustion herself.

One day in late May a letter came from Papa. Mama gathered everyone around Bud and read the letter out loud. It was just the key that unlocked Bud's mind. Papa wrote of all the preparations that were being made in Corinth. The Union force that had pushed the Rebels out of Shiloh were on the march to attack them. Union General Halleck, who was superior to Grant, had arrived on the scene in western Tennessee and was now in charge of the movement to Corinth. Papa believed the Army of the Mississippi was greatly outnumbered, although Beauregard was declaring that his army was being strongly reinforced. Day and night Rebel soldiers worked non-stop, digging entrenchments, gathering supplies, and strengthening lines. When the Yankees attacked, and Papa was sure they would, the Rebels would be ready.

Bud listened intently to the information. He asked Mama to read the letter again and then once more. He looked at the faces around him as if seeing them all for the first time. Then, to everyone's surprise, he pulled back the bedcovers and attempted to stand. His legs were weak from lying so long, but Mama and Suzanna supported him on each side and helped him down the stairs. He wanted to see his horse Lightning, but the walk to the barn was much too far and difficult in his condition. So Josup brought the horse to the back porch, and Bud stroked his long head and mane.

Later that night, Bud sat at the dining table for the first time, and after a delicious supper, he began to talk. Much like Papa did, Bud spoke of the noise, the confusion, the heat, and the smoke of the battlefield. His mind was like a dam that had been broken, and everything was gushing out. He talked of rushing up the ridge on which the Yankees had been camped and seeing them run. He told about the Rebels who had eaten their breakfasts right out of the Yankees' skillets. He described the thirst and the smoke and tired, aching bones as they charged, again and again, the enemy in the sunken road. Mama, Suzanna, and Rachel listened without interruption, sometimes grimacing, other times shaking their heads in disbelief. But they did not sob until Bud told them about a boy named Jimmy, the color-bearer, who had carried their magnificent flag so bravely until he went down. It was the last thing Bud remembered from that awful day.

When Bud was finished, sniffling was all that could be heard for a long time. Then Suzanna moved quietly to Bud, and they embraced. Mama smiled. They all knew that Bud was a changed man forever. In truth, they were all changed forever, but Bud had finally thrown off the blanket of trauma that had nearly smothered him.

By June Bud had regained much of his strength. He had long since gotten rid of the bandage and sling for his arm. Working hard at exercising the injured arm, he was soon lifting and carrying things again. He rode his horse daily and helped Mama oversee the slaves and other jobs that had to be done.

A wire came by messenger early on the morning of June second. Union troops were in full force right outside Corinth. Although Beauregard had carried out an elaborate ruse pretending that reinforcements were pouring into the Confederate lines, he was convinced the Union army would attack and knew that, in fact, his men were badly outnumbered. Beauregard also knew they could not survive a siege if it came to that, so he pulled back all troops from Corinth, farther south, to Tupelo. When the Yankees made their charge, much to their surprise, the town was empty of all Rebels. Corinth was taken without a fight.

Bud fumed at the news. How could Beauregard have given up Corinth without a fight? It was infuriating to him. Not only had they retreated from Shiloh back to their starting point, now the Rebel army was farther away from Tennessee than before. It was then that Bud announced his intentions to return to his company.

What protests arose on hearing this! Suzanna pleaded with Bud not to go back just yet. After all, the damage was done, and there wasn't anything going on in Tupelo.

183

Mama insisted he was not yet well enough for camp life. So, the matter was closed, temporarily.

The next day brought a letter from Papa. It was short but bore good news. Papa had just received word that he had been promoted to the rank of colonel. Looking around at all the smiling faces, Mama proclaimed how very proud she was. But her face betrayed the fear she felt inside. More importance in the Confederate army only meant more danger from the Federals.

A second wire for Bud arrived the very next day. This one also bore good news. Bud had been promoted as well. He was now a captain. This was the last straw. Bud could stay at home no longer, and the women knew it. There were no protests, no demands, but many tears.

As the Franklin women watched Bud gallop away, they knew they had been lucky in this past conflict. They wished they could believe that the worst was over, but they knew in their hearts that the worst was yet to come.

11

The Journal

december 31, 1863

RACHEL SIGHED AND CLOSED HER JOURNAL. Dark shadows danced on the walls from the flickering lamp on her bedside table. She rubbed her tired eyes and listened. The house was silent except for the clock ticking in the hall and an occasional pop or creak of the wooden floor. It was very late, and everyone in the house was asleep.

After supper Rachel had retired to her room to write in her journal; Mama insisted. She had just finished the last entry of the year, dated December 31, 1862, and was planning to re-join Mama and Suzanna downstairs. As she closed the journal she had absent-mindedly thumbed through the wrinkled pages and found herself reading with great interest the events of the year through which they had all lived… and survived.

The year 1862 had started badly. As Rachel read she remembered the hurried wedding and the hasty departure of Papa and Bud. But, if the year started badly, it had only gotten worse. The Battle of Shiloh was the first bloody conflict of the year, but by no means the last one. After the tally was made 1,732 Confederate men were killed in the two-day battle. Wounded and missing numbered almost 9,000. The Federals had fared no better with 1,754 killed, about 12,000 wounded and missing. The devastation had shocked both sides of the country so terribly that it would seem the great leaders, the people themselves, would have put a stop to the madness.

But, Shiloh seemed to have only set the standard for other battles that followed. Throughout the summer of 1862 war raged furiously in Virginia. General McClellan finally decided to venture out of his 'burrow' and move on Richmond, the capital city and 'heart' of the Confederacy. To cut out the heart would cause the death of the remaining parts, and that was his plan. He set his troops in motion by transporting them by water to the tip end of the Virginia Peninsula. Protected by the James River on one side and the York River on the other, he planned to march 75 miles to Richmond. On the last day of May his army ran up against General Joe Johnston's Rebel force at a place called Seven Pines. It was in this battle that the second Confederate general named Johnston, although no relation to the first, was wounded. Unlike A.S. Johnston, Joe Johnston did not die but had to be relieved of command to recuperate.

Little did southern people know then, but this was a heaven-sent twist of fate. For in his place came the most beloved Confederate general of the war, no less the most respected in all of history, General Robert E. Lee. Lee took command of the Army of Northern Virginia and pushed McClellan's army back down the peninsula in what was called The Seven Days Battle. This was Lee's first great feat of the war, but it was accomplished with great loss of life.

Rachel had not written much about battles in her journal. Mama, of course, kept up with all the action and explained it to her in simple terms. But, ever since Bud's experience at Shiloh, Rachel had not wanted to think about or write about any more battles. However, she had devoted a whole page to the revered General Lee.

Neither Rachel nor Mama had ever seen Robert E. Lee, but Rachel overheard her mother say that he was a very handsome fellow. Mrs. Varena Davis, wife of the Confederate president, had written Mama a letter describing the general in some detail. She wrote that his dark, brown eyes were the softest she had ever seen, and his manner was supremely gentlemanly. General Lee was soft-spoken as well and as true-blue a Virginian if ever there was one. In fact, Lee had been asked by General Winfield Scott, commander-in-chief of the U.S. armed forces, to be commander of the Union army, but he had turned down the offer, stating that he could never fight against his home

state of Virginia. It did not take long for Robert E. Lee to rise so high on the southern pedestal that people believed they could not touch the heel of his boot.

As Rachel turned the page, her eyes fell upon a date at the top of the page, August twelfth. She remembered that day well. It had been a dark, grievous day. Mr. Gunther had just been on their back porch two days before discussing with Mama that Henry had run off to the war again. Everyone had expected Henry to do so, even sooner than he did, but Mr. Gunther was keeping his head this time and not trying to fetch his son back. But what happened after that no one expected. Poor, crazy Mrs. Gunther had disappeared the following night, probably looking for her son. She was found the next day, August twelfth, by her husband, face down in the bayou, and so her search and her misery were ended. She now rested in the small cemetery beside the church. Rachel grimaced as she thought again how terrible to be drowned in the bayou. She quickly turned to the next page.

There she read a brief entry on a second battle at Bull Run Creek, or Manassas Junction, in Virginia. Rachel thought it very odd that the armies would fight at the same place almost a year and a month later. And with much the same result. The Federal Army of Virginia, now led by General John Pope (George McClellan having been called back to Washington after his failure to take Richmond) was faced with Lee's Army of Northern Virginia and two of its great leaders, 'Stonewall' Jackson and James Longstreet. Together, they were successful in pushing Pope's men away from Bull Run Creek and back to the safety of Washington, a repeat performance of the previous year.

By the end of the summer of 1862 there seemed to be no end to hardships. All but one of the important port cities along the Mississippi from Memphis to New Orleans were under Union control. Only Vicksburg was still in Confederate hands and holding out with all its might. How long this would last was anybody's guess, for General Grant was in Memphis busily working on a plan to take it. He was frustrated but not undaunted, and that was dangerous for the South.

With ports closed to the South the price of goods had risen unbelievably high. Sugar and salt were as precious as gold. Flour, coffee, tea were now luxuries instead of daily fare. New shoes were out of the question as well as new dresses, hats, and gloves. Everyone, rich and poor alike, were learning how to do without. It was as if Papa had gazed into a crystal ball when he had predicted last fall that the shortages were sure to happen.

But, Papa had not prepared them for the biggest hardship of all. With the Yankees army residing in much of west Tennessee and parts of northern Mississippi the slaves were smelling their chance for freedom. At first the slaves began to trickle away, one or two at a time, in search of the Yankee camp. But, soon whole families and large groups disappeared from their slave quarters. Only the few who were too afraid to run into the unknown or those who felt they could not leave the only

place that had ever been home were left to harvest the crops and work the plantations.

The Franklins felt lucky that only a small number of their slaves had run. But, even then, it became apparent that, as appalling as it seemed at first, all hands would be needed to get in the bountiful cotton. Otherwise, the bolls would rot in the fields, and, as everyone knew, things were too desperate to let that happen. Cotton was all they had.

All the terrible memories came flooding back as Rachel read about that morning in late September when Mama had awakened her before dawn. Only Lily had been spared the back-breaking work of picking in the fields so she could cook and see after the house. Even then, she had fussed the loudest.

"What dis worl' comin' to when missus hab to pick cot'n!" Lily ranted as she prepared breakfast.

What *had* the world come to Rachel had thought to herself as she set her floppy hat on her head and followed Mama and Suzanna to the field. They each draped a long burlap sack over one shoulder and began their work. Everyone was silent in the semi-darkness of dawn. Mama showed Rachel and Lizbet how to pluck the soft cotton from the hull, and then she moved quickly to another row to fill her own sack. Suzanna was several rows over with Jo and Mott beyond her. But soon they had all moved out of sight, picking much faster than Rachel and Lizbet, and hidden from view by the tall cotton stalks.

Lizbet, who was prone to move drag-foot on difficult tasks and do a fair amount of fussing like her mother, decided to stop right there between the rows and take a rest. Rachel had scolded her severely, but it did no good.

"Dis cot'n-pickin' make my head hurt," she had grumbled from her seat on the ground.

Rachel had simply called out from somewhere down the row. "Well, if a black racer or cotton-mouth comes to call, don't yell for help. We won't hear you."

That had ended Lizbet's rest and her headache. She didn't stay far from Rachel after that.

Rachel stopped reading for awhile. She laid her head on the journal and thought about the cotton fields. The sun had beat down on them unmercifully. She remembered the sweat rolling down her face and neck, and the pestering mosquitoes and gnats that swarmed around her. She could almost feel the burning ache of her back and shoulders from the constant bending and pulling on the heavy cotton sack. But, worst of all were her fingers. The sharp hulls tore into her soft skin, and she would jerk back her hands, cut and bleeding.

Many nights Rachel had been so tired she had fallen to sleep without supper. Every morning she was too stiff to get out of bed. Her fingers were too swollen and sore to move, but she knew she had no choice. As long as her mother worked like a slave Rachel would be right there with her. It had made Rachel sad to think about her mother, so genteel and delicate, having to labor so hard in the fields. Life was no longer about comfort and pleasure; it was now all about survival.

Just then, Mama peeked her head in Rachel's door, snapping her out of her daydreaming.

"Are you all right, dear?" she asked softly.

"Yes, ma'am," Rachel smiled at her mother. "I'm just readin' my journal."

Mama moved inside the room and sat on Rachel's bed. She put her hand on Rachel's soft hair and looked at the book.

"My goodness," she remarked when she saw how thick the journal was. "You've really been busy this year."

Rachel nodded. "Yes, ma'am, there was a lot to write about."

Mama nodded in agreement. Then they both sat awhile in silence, thinking about the past months, the coming new year, and life in general.

Finally Mama spoke up. "Let's pray that the new year brings Papa and Bud home soon...and that this ugly... dreadful war will be over."

Then she stood up, kissed Rachel on the head, and bid her good-night.

Rachel sighed. If only the war would end, all their worries, their problems, would end as well. Rachel sat up and pulled the quilt tightly around her as the room was getting really cold. Then she went back to reading in her journal.

There were long gaps in time, skipping several days here and more than a week there. The pages that had been written were only a paragraph or two, but Rachel knew the reason for this. Her days of picking cotton were too long and tiresome, her fingers too sore to hold a pen. But, she did come across an entry dated September 30, 1862.

It briefly described another horrible battle. This time the fighting had occurred in Maryland at a town

called Sharpsburg. Lee's Army of Northern Virginia had crossed the Potomac River into Maryland. General George McClellan was back on the scene with a newly organized force, the Army of the Potomac, nearly 90,000 strong. The fighting here began on the morning of September 17th and proved to be the bloodiest single day of the war. One Union general, in particular, gained fame from this day. His name was General Ambrose Burnside. It was his job to get his men across a small bridge that spanned Antietam Creek and wipe out the Rebels on the other side. After two bloody repulses, Burnside charged a third time and finally succeeded in getting on the Rebel side. Heavily outnumbering the Confederates the Yankees pushed them back until Rebel reinforcements came and reversed the tide. By battle's end Burnside was back again at Antietam Creek, having gained no ground at all. During the night General Lee decided it was wiser to retreat to Virginia than resume the battle a second day.

Rachel sighed. All this fighting, back and forth, with nobody really winning. There was little to show for all the struggle except a huge loss of life. She didn't understand war at all. She couldn't see how it would ever end. When all the men were dead? Maybe that was it. She slowly turned the page.

Not everything written in the journal was as unhappy as it might seem. Rachel read the next page and giggled out loud. October 10, 1862, was an unforgettable day for Rachel. Laura Millbrook and her darling baby, John-John, had made an unexpected visit. Miss Laura had come to see about her own house that she had left when Evan went off to war. Evan and she had planned to move back just as soon as Evan was fully recuperated. Who knew when that would be, Evan was having such a hard time with it, but wouldn't it be grand to be close again! Miss Laura was always so bubbly!

If Miss Laura had been shocked to see the Franklin women slaving in the fields, she didn't show it. All over the South, people were doing things they never expected to do in a million years. But, what a wonderful break from the cotton!

John Evan Millbrook III was a beautiful baby, blonde and blue-eyed just like his mother. He was almost a year old and was tottering around in a funny, duck-like waddle. Rachel laughed when he suddenly plopped on his bottom, and John-John laughed at her. All the women made quite a fuss over him all day and the next. When it was time for Miss Laura to leave they could hardly bear it, especially Rachel who had grown extremely attached to the precious baby. Too soon, the cooing, the laughing, the giggling were replaced with groaning and grunting and sighing as they all returned to the fields.

By mid-October good progress had been made in clearing the fields of cotton, but there was still an overwhelming amount of work for worn-out hands and bodies. Everyone was near total exhaustion, and Mama couldn't ignore the obvious. Finally accepting that the job was much too daunting for them, she went in search of help. She managed to borrow some slaves from neighboring farms, and for the first time in over a month, Rachel and Suzanna had been able to sit in the parlor and re-read Bud's letters. Sewing or playing the piano was out of the question with their sore fingers.

New shoes. There, she had read it again. How many times had Rachel written that she wanted new shoes? It wasn't a question of fashion but dire necessity. Months ago she had worn a hole in the sole of her shoe. Lily had repaired it with a leather patch, but soon after Rachel's feet had a growing spurt, and her toes were being pinched something awful. Mama had given Rachel a pair of her shoes, but they were too big, and Rachel had to wear them stuffed with cotton in the toes. Rachel's birthday was coming soon, and all she had wished for was a new pair of shoes.

Rachel got the shoes. They weren't exactly new, and it was a sad day when she received them. A week before Rachel's twelfth birthday, Suzanna's mother died. Suzanna had wept so hard, but through the tears she kept repeating that it was really a blessing. Her mother had been extremely ill for such a long time, and now she was at rest, no longer in pain. Rachel cried because she couldn't bear to see Suzanna cry. Bud could not be there to comfort his wife, and that made things even worse.

Bud was somewhere in northeastern Tennessee near Knoxville. He had left Mississippi back in June with General Braxton Bragg in command. Beauregard had taken a leave of absence immediately following Shiloh and had not been seen since. Bragg's army was re-named the Army of Tennessee, and they had headed for that state, Chattanooga in particular, to take control of the city before Buell's Federals arrived. They lost the race with Buell to Chattanooga, so Bud's army was marched north into Kentucky.

Buell's Army of the Ohio went after them, meeting up in a Kentucky town called Perryville. Fighting occurred on October 8th with Buell attacking a Confederate force less than a third the size of his own. However, when the smoke cleared the battle was considered a Confederate victory. Buell had been unable to overtake the smaller force, and the next day, October 9th, Bragg's army had gotten away. They had escaped capture, or worse yet, annihilation, with all their supplies and guns intact. The Rebels made it back to Knoxville in one piece, though minus the 510 who had been killed and 251 captured, not to mention the 2,635 who had been wounded.

Bud had survived the battle unscathed this time. He had hardly mentioned the conflict in his letter, but Mama had read all the details in the newspaper some days after it happened. It had horrified them to think that Bud had once more been in such grave danger. Papa was not with him this time but somewhere in west Tennessee near Memphis. Neither had come home since leaving in June, and the prospect of them coming home anytime soon was glum.

So, Suzanna buried her mother with only Uncle Phillip, Mama, and Rachel by her side. It was a sad day, indeed, to see Suzanna so grief-stricken. She stayed in her

mother's house in town for several days, and when she returned she had a wagonful of goods, boxes, crates, bags filled with clothes, bolts of material, coffee, flour, tea, and shoes. Rachel's eyes lit up when she saw the shoes. Mrs. Wade was a very petite lady, just Rachel's size in fact, and the shoes were a perfect fit. Suzanna smiled as she handed Rachel a box with several pairs, three, maybe four, almost brand new, beautiful shoes.

Rachel hesitated as she eyed the box. After all, these belonged to Suzanna's mother, and Rachel didn't feel right about taking them.

"They're yours," Suzanna had urged, pushing the box into Rachel's arms. "Please, take them. My mother would want you to have them. Please."

Rachel had thanked Suzanna and run as fast as she could to her room to try them on. The guilty feeling soon was swept away as she discarded Mama's old misfit shoes and strutted around with her new ones which felt wonderful to her tortured feet.

The guilty feeling crept over Rachel even now as she read about the new shoes. She had also inherited some new dresses, two hats, and several pairs of gloves that she needed badly. Mama had assured her it was all right to wear Mrs. Wade's things. Mama had taken many needed items as well: linens, cloth, blankets, and of course, the food. These were bad times, and it was not sensible to be too proud to accept things that they needed. Besides, Suzanna had said that her mother was smiling down from heaven to see Rachel so happy and pretty in her clothes.

Just then, Rachel heard the clock in the hallway strike twelve. The new year had come. How odd and solemn it was! There were no cheers, no celebrations, little hope for the year 1863. The old year had been one crisis after another. Fear and anxiety were constant companions. Death and misery blanketed the whole nation. Thousands of men had been killed in the struggles that marked 1862. How many more would follow only time would tell. The future did not look promising.

12
The Yankees Are Comin'!

january, 1863

MAMA THREW DOWN THE NEWSPAPER in a huff. She was more than disgusted; she was downright mad. Mama, Suzanna, and Rachel had been quietly reading in the parlor, Suzanna absorbed in a book of poetry, Rachel re-reading *Jane Eyre*, a wonderfully romantic love story. Mama had been reading an account of another terrible battle that had taken place before Christmas, December 13th to be exact.

"What's wrong, Mama?" Rachel asked.

"Oh, it's this war," Mama fumed. "The senseless killing. It becomes more and more brutal with every battle, and I can hardly *stand* it."

"What were you reading?" Suzanna asked, very concerned. "Was it about Bud's company?"

Mama shook her head. "No, no, I'm sorry, dear. I didn't mean to alarm you. I was reading about Fredericksburg, you remember, we heard of it right before Christmas in Virginia."

"Did we lose, Mama?" asked Rachel innocently.

"No, actually it was an overwhelming victory for us," Mama tried to explain. "I just... I just don't understand how these Yankee generals can have such little regard for the lives of their men. They seem to care less for their men than the enemy."

Now Rachel was confused. "What do you mean, Mama? What happened?"

"Well," Mama began. "As you know, General McClellan was replaced by General Ambrose Burnside of Antietam fame. Burnside's only goal was to get Robert E. Lee, and to do so, he had to cross the Rappahannock River where Lee's forces were concentrated on the opposite side. The problem was that Lee's men were strongly entrenched on higher ground just past the town of Fredericksburg. But, the Federals continued to charge the Rebel lines that could not be broken. At a particular spot, Marye's Heights, the Yankees were faced with charging across open ground while our men, above them on the heights, poured gunfire down upon them. They didn't have a chance, you see. Yet, Burnside continued to order assault after assault, and all with the same result. It was a slaughter, nothing but a slaughter. It's all so dreadful, so senseless."

Mama put her hands to her face. Rachel thought Mama might be crying, but in a few seconds, she dropped her hands and lifted her chin. The weariness and worry showed in every inch of her beautiful face.

"Well, I'm sorry, dear. You didn't really need to hear that," Mama apologized. "It's just… well, it upsets me so at times."

It was also bad timing. They had just received news about Bud's unit being in a fight on the very first day of the new year, of all things. Bragg's army had moved out of Knoxville right before Christmas to Stones River near Murfreesboro, Tennessee, just southeast of Nashville. Papa had written that he had also moved to this location, so once again father and son were fighting together.

As it seemed customary for the Union, General Buell had been replaced due to his bad performance at Perryville. In command now was General William 'Old Rosy' Rosecrans, and the army under his command was renamed the Army of the Cumberland. Rachel thought it awfully silly how the Union couldn't make up their minds who was going to be general or what they wanted to call their armies.

December 30th found the two armies face to face, both having plans to attack the following day. General Bragg's men got the jump by attacking at the crack of dawn on the 31st. This was almost disastrous for the Yankees, and they were pushed back to the Nashville Turnpike. Only the setting sun saved Rosecrans' army that day.

The next day, New Year's Day, there was no fighting

at all. But, on the afternoon of the 2nd the Confederates went in for the kill. In their enthusiasm the charging Rebels went beyond their intended position and were mowed down by Union guns. Nearly 1,500 men were killed or wounded within a few minutes. The survivors went running back to their lines, and the Battle of Stones River was over. On January 3rd, Bragg withdrew to Tullahoma, thirty-six miles to the south.

Of course, Mama had read all the gory details from the papers. Neither Papa nor Bud would write such worrisome news. It was enough for the Franklin women to hear that their two men had made it safely out of the battle. Mama, Suzanna, and Rachel rejoiced and thanked the Lord together. Silently, they each knew in their hearts that the odds were closing in on Papa and Bud. They feared that each day would bring a new battle, and one or both of them would not be so lucky.

Slowly, the cold winter months turned into spring. The days of April were breezy and warm as Mama, Suzanna, and Rachel planted the garden. Mr. Gunther was doing the best he could with the many acres to be planted in cotton, and few hands to do it. Mama sighed and told him to do as much as he could. If things didn't change, they wouldn't be able to pick it all come next fall anyway. There had been no word from Papa or Bud in weeks, and no hope that they would be home soon.

Rachel straightened up from hoeing the garden dirt. She stretched her back and rubbed her eyes. Then she saw a man's figure coming across the yard toward the garden.

The man was somewhat bow-legged and had a stooped, swaggering walk. Rachel knew right away who it was.

"Mama, Mr. Yancey's comin'," Rachel said.

Mr. Yancey had made it his duty to check on the Franklin household every few days. He knew how difficult it was for women to run a plantation alone, not to mention, how dangerous.

"Mornin', Belle," Mr. Yancey called as he approached.

"Good morning, John," she answered. "How's Camille today?"

"About the same, thank ya," he grunted. "About the same."

Since Robert had been killed at Shiloh, Mrs. Yancey had taken to her bed, drapes drawn, lying day after day in the darkness of her room. She would not even get up to take meals or bathe herself. It was sad, very sad.

"My, Miss Rachel, you're as pretty as a picture. Look more like your mother every day," Mr. Yancey commented. He said the same thing to Rachel almost every time he saw her. Rachel smiled and thanked him for the compliment. Then he nodded to Suzanna who was on the far side of the garden. "Mornin' Miss Suzanna. You're lookin' well today."

Suzanna returned the greeting with a smile and went back to hoeing.

Then Mr. Yancey turned his attention to Mama and looked serious.

"Belle, any word from William?" he asked.

Mama shook her head 'no.' Then Mr. Yancey did an odd thing.

"Come walk with me," he said to Mama. She understood that he wanted to get out of listening range of young ears.

Suzanna and Rachel exchanged puzzled looks. Rachel strained to hear what Mr. Yancey was saying as Mama and he strolled toward the house.

"There's been news..." his voice faded in and out. "Comin' through here... stay close, Belle..."

Then Rachel thought she heard something about a gun and keep it loaded. Her heart pounded as she imagined what could be happening. They had been hearing horrible rumors about the Yankees riding into towns and single plantations, pillaging and stealing and burning buildings. It had been her worst fear: Yankees on their land, in their house. Nothing would be left for them after the northern *locusts* swarmed through. It was an unthinkable nightmare.

When Mr. Yancey left, Mama returned to the garden, picked up her hoe, and resumed her work without saying a word. Suzanna and Rachel waited patiently for Mama to explain what was going on, but Mama didn't offer an explanation. Finally, Rachel could keep quiet no longer.

"Mama, what did Mr. Yancey say?"

Mama looked up with a most solemn expression on her face, but she did not speak.

Then Suzanna spoke up. "Please, Mrs. Franklin, please tell us. We need to know."

Mama sighed. She knew Suzanna was right. She dropped her hoe.

"Let's go sit in the shade," was her answer.

Just as they reached the big oak, Lily came out with a pitcher of cool water. They sat awhile in the shade and again waited patiently for Mama to speak.

"Mr. Yancey says he's heard news that a Yankee raiding party is headed this way," Mama spoke calmly and quietly. "Cavalry under the command of a Colonel Grierson, one of Grant's best."

Mama saw the looks of dread on the two younger faces turn to looks of horror.

"Now, don't be too alarmed," Mama reassured them. "They could be riding miles away from here by now. These Union men have put themselves in a lot of danger by venturing so far from their lines. Our men can overtake them easily. It was just a warning. You know Mr. Yancey. He's a dear, but overly cautious most of the time."

Mama smiled to show her lack of concern for the news. Suzanna and Rachel smiled in accord, but all three women were inwardly scared to death.

Before the sun would rise on another day, they would indeed be more scared than they had ever been before.

13

Face to Face

april, 1863

"Amen," Mama ended the blessing before supper. Rachel opened her eyes and looked at her food. The bountiful meals she remembered from the past were replaced by simple, vegetable and cornbread ones. Sometimes there was pork or chicken, but meat was more of a treat than usual fare.

Mama had taken over Papa's seat at the head of the table long ago with Rachel and Suzanna sitting on each side of her. But tonight Suzanna's place was empty. Sometime shortly after Mr. Yancey's visit, Suzanna had become ill. She was running a fever and shivering with chills, and now she lay upstairs in her bed. This worried Rachel and Mama, as Suzanna had been sickly a lot this past winter.

They were both thinking of Mrs. Wade, so frail and weak, and hoped Suzanna was not taking after her mother. If she was no better in the morning, Mama would fetch Dr. Prentiss to see about her.

So far this day, everything had been quiet and normal. Mama had not entirely disregarded Mr. Yancey's warning as Lily and she had spent the afternoon putting more things in secret panels and false walls. There were more treasures stuffed and hidden throughout the house and grounds that Rachel wondered if they would ever find them again.

Mama was dishing out warm potatoes onto Rachel's plate when, suddenly, in a matter of seconds, the whole world seemed to spin out of control. It began with an ear-piercing scream from Lily and a loud commotion in the back of the house. Mama leaped up and ran for the kitchen. Rachel was right behind her, but she heard her mother scream before she could see what was happening. Rachel felt herself being pushed against the wall. Lily, Mama, and Josup were huddled around someone, and they were all trying to hold up the body.

Rachel finally realized that the body was Papa. His arm was draped over Josup's back as the much smaller Josup was trying to drag Papa into the hall. Mama and Lily were helping him support the heavy weight, and everyone was stumbling and shaking and giving orders.

Rachel stood up against the wall to stay out of the way. She couldn't believe what she was seeing. There was a trail of blood across the kitchen floor where Papa had been dragged in. She began to tremble and cry. Then she tore herself away from the wall and ran after her father.

The small group had made it half-way up the stairs. Papa groaned, but his eyes were closed, and Rachel knew he was unconscious. She watched his heavy boots drag on the steps as they lifted and tugged and finally got Papa to the top of the stairs. As they laid Papa on his bed he awoke and began to shout,

"There's no time, Belle! There's no time!"

Mama was hushing him as he gasped and tried to speak.

"No, Belle," he struggled with each breath. "They're right behind me... they're after me... and they'll be... here... any minute."

Rachel crept to the door of her parents' room. She had to see if Papa was all right, but then she wished she hadn't. When Mama pulled back his jacket, there was a large, dark spot on his shirt, right above the waist on his left side. Papa was shot. Rachel let out a scream, but either it was not as loud as she thought or everyone was so busy they did not hear her.

"Run fetch Dr. Prentiss!" Mama shrieked to Josup who made for the door.

"No! I say. No!" Papa raised up from the bed as if to tackle Josup before he reached the door. He grabbed Mama by the arm and shook her. "Listen to me... listen."

Everyone froze. Papa lay back on the pillow. He was trying to catch his breath.

"I have important orders... for my men," Papa gasped. His chest was heaving and jerking as he tried to breathe. He coughed and began again. "I have to get these orders to my men... someone must take them."

Mama looked at Lily and Josup. They all had stunned looks on their faces and absolutely no idea what to do.

"The Yankees are after me," Papa managed to calm down somewhat. His breathing was steadier now. "They'll be here any minute."

Now Rachel was breathing in heavy jerks. Her worst fears had come true. The Yankees were going to be on their land, in their home. And what about Papa? What would they do to Papa when they found him? They were sure to find him. He couldn't be moved in his condition. And what would they do to all the rest of them as well? Rachel's head began to spin, and she thought she might faint.

But, that was out of the question right now. Papa needed everyone. She had to keep a clear head. If they only knew what to do.

Mama knew what to do. As soon as she understood what was happening, she set everyone into motion. Lily was to get the girls, Jo and Mott and Lizbet to clean up the bloody mess in the kitchen, the porch, the stairs. No trace of blood must be seen. Lily was to return with clean linen, a bowl of water, and towels. Josup was to hide Papa's horse, not in the stable, but down by the bayou behind the slave cabins. And Rachel, quick dear, bring me the scissors from that drawer.

Mama began cutting Papa's shirt where the bloodstain was. As she peeled back the bloody cloth Rachel could see a small hole, pulsing dark red and oozing blood. It reminded Rachel of Bud's sickening wound, and she felt she might be sick again. But, this time there was no time to be sick. The Yankees were coming.

Lily ran in with the materials for cleaning and bandaging Papa's wounds. Papa was talking softly to Mama the whole time she was wiping and dabbing. Rachel saw her mother reach into her father's coat pocket and pull out a small paper. She knew it must be the orders Papa had raved about. Mama slipped the paper down the front of her blouse. Just let the Yankees look there, she dared.

Just as Mama had finished wrapping the last clean strips of cloth around and around Papa's waist Josup came running into the room, out of breath, and panting.

"Dey's comin', Miz Belle, dey's comin'!" he yelled.

Everyone froze and listened. The sound of hoof beats could be heard galloping down the lane. Mama quickly stood up and looked around. She was thinking hard as her temples throbbed and her jaws clenched tightly together. Then she had it. She pointed to an oversized trunk that Suzanna that brought from her house and was still sitting in the hall.

"Quick, Lily!" she snapped. "Empty everything out of that trunk. Put the things in a drawer or closet. Use Suzanna's room."

Lily moved with lightning speed, pulling bedsheets and blankets from the large trunk. Then Mama turned her attention to Josup.

"Josup, quick, go get a knife," she ordered. Josup began to fumble in his pocket and pulled out a fairly large one. He pulled out the blade and to their surprise, it was as big as his hand and sharpened to a fine edge. Rachel wondered where he had gotten such a weapon, but no matter, she was glad he had it.

"Cut some holes in the back of that trunk," she demanded, "about the size of a hen's egg."

Josup looked puzzled, but he asked no questions. He immediately got to work on the trunk.

The sound of horses' hooves grew louder, and Mama snuffed out the lamp that was beside the bed.

"Rachel, come here, dear," Mama said softly. She was exceptionally calm under such deadly circumstances. "Help me move your father."

Papa's eyes were closed, and he may have passed out again. But the jostling he was receiving soon revived him.

"Sweetheart, take his arm here," Mama was lifting Papa off the bed by wrapping his right arm over her shoulder. Rachel slipped in and put her body under his left side, trying hard not to touch the fresh bandage. Together they managed to get Papa upright, but his weight was almost more than they could bear. Suddenly, the sound of horses was directly under their window. They could hear the animals snort, and the men shout at each other.

This gave Mama and Rachel a supernatural strength. They carried Papa across the room and down the hall. With Josup to help, the three of them lifted Papa's long legs and sat him down in the trunk. There was a terribly loud banging on the back door. The Yankees were here!

Mama pushed Papa's head over onto his knees. For a brief moment they looked into each other's eyes, fearing it might be for the last time. Mama quickly kissed Papa on the head and closed the trunk lid.

Just in time! The soldiers had come into the house. They could hear boots tromping downstairs in the hall, in the parlor, in the dining room. Rachel's heart was racing. She looked at Mama for courage. Mama gave her a warm, reassuring smile and nodded her head as if to say 'everything'll be fine.'

Rachel wished she could believe that. She was so afraid her eyes would give away the secret. A nervous glance at the trunk under the scrupulous eyes of a sly Yankee might just give Papa's hiding place away. She tried hard to look calm and brave like her mother in the face of the enemy. But, it was impossible for her to do.

Mama looked at Josup, and her eyes got big. His shirt was bloodstained and dirty. The Yankees couldn't see him like that! Mama waved Josup into Suzanna's room where he could change into one of Bud's shirts. Not only did Josup change his shirt, but he slipped out Suzanna's open window, taking his stained shirt with him, and disappeared. Rachel hoped he had not fallen from the second-story window and broken a bone, but there was no

time to think about him now.

Soon the noisy boots started up the stairs. The first Yankee officer stopped short, startled to see Mama standing defiantly at the top of the stairs. There were four or five other Yankees behind him. They all stared at the three women, Mama, Lily, and Rachel, who were staring right back at them.

Instinctively, the first officer tipped his hat as a courtesy to the women. Mama made no sign that she noticed. Her face was stone-cold. The Yankee was young and broad-shouldered with a neatly trimmed moustache. Rachel may have thought him handsome if he weren't a Yankee.

"You must be Mrs. Franklin, lady of the house," the soldier said politely.

Mama did not answer but lifted her proud chin even more.

The Yankee officer only smiled. He had run up against southern women before and was not surprised at this reception. He looked beyond Mama to where Rachel was standing with Lily and smiled again. Even the young ones were just like their mothers, so proud, so obstinate, but so pretty.

"I'm Captain Ross with Grierson's cavalry," he introduced himself. He rested his hand on his saber and continued. "We've come for your husband, Colonel William Franklin."

"My husband, sir, is not here," Mama answered coldly.

Captain Ross merely smiled again. "Well, if you would oblige us, ma'am, we would like to see for ourselves."

He started up the rest of the way to the top of the stairs with the others following closely. Mama made no move to get out of their way but stood firm until the captain came eye to eye with her.

"Ma'am, if you don't mind," he said in an overly polite manner.

Mama knew he was mocking her, and she took a few steps back to let them pass.

It was hard to watch as the men intruded into their rooms, looking at their things, and poking around in their belongings. Rachel's fear was momentarily replaced by anger. How dare these vile Yankees burst into their home!

One soldier started into Suzanna's room, and Mama could no longer remain silent.

"Don't go in there!" Mama insisted. All the soldiers stopped, thinking they had hit upon their prisoner. The captain came rushing into the hall from Rachel's room to see what the commotion was all about. Mama looked at him, her eyes somewhat softer now, and said,

"My daughter-in-law is in that room," she was almost pleading. "She's very sick. Please do not disturb her." Then as an after-thought she added, "We think it's typhoid."

The captain froze in his tracks, and the soldier who had entered Suzanna's room stepped back quickly. They wanted no part of typhoid or any other deadly disease. Captain Ross nodded his okay to the other men, and they left Suzanna's room untouched.

217

Although only a few minutes had passed while the Yankees ransacked their rooms, it seemed like hours. Mama, Rachel, and Lily stood motionless the whole while trying not to look at the trunk. They were so afraid Papa might groan and give himself away. If only the soldiers would hurry!

Then, finally, the captain seemed satisfied that their man was not upstairs. As they filed down the stairs Rachel began to breathe easier. But, all at once, the captain swung around and eyed the trunk. He stared at Mama, then Lily, and last of all, Rachel, looking for any small, tell-tale sign in their eyes that someone might be hiding there.

"Open that trunk," he ordered Lily who was standing closest to it. Her face went blank, and her eyes deadened, the look that slaves were so good at. She didn't move a muscle. As cool as could be, Mama stepped over to the trunk and stood in front of it.

"This is my private trunk," Mama said without flinching. "There's nothing in it of any interest to you."

"Well, I think I'll decide for myself," was his answer. "Open it."

Mama stood her ground. Her green eyes stared coolly at the captain, and her chin lifted high.

"No, sir, I will not open the trunk," she replied.

Now Rachel's heart was pounding so hard, she could hear it in her head. She was so afraid for her mother she could not breathe. Sure that Papa was going to be discovered, she could hardly stand still.

Sensing Rachel's uneasiness, Lily had moved behind

her and was holding onto her sash to keep her in place. From their position facing Mama and the trunk, they could see the tiny trickle of blood that had begun to seep out of the back of it. The blood was slowly easing along the floorboard. Soon it would be in view of the captain.

Again, Captain Ross ordered Mama to open the trunk, and again she refused. It was becoming a contest of wills. The other men had stopped and were watching from the bottom of the stairs. Aware of his need to press his authority lest he be ridiculed by his subordinates, Captain Ross did an unthinkable thing.

He pulled his pistol on Mama.

Rachel jerked against Lily's grip to rush to her mother and beg her to obey the captain. But Lily twisted tighter, nearly cutting off Rachel's circulation around her waist. Rachel was unable to move. She watched in sheer disbelief. The blood was still creeping on the floor, and the gun was still pointed at Mama. Both her parents were facing death.

Mama stood even calmer and more steadfast than before. She looked the captain squarely in the eyes, her green eyes never faltering, never acknowledging the muzzle that was pointing directly at her.

"You'll have to shoot then," was Mama's answer. "I will not open the trunk." Rachel gasped and Lily pulled tighter.

This was not what the captain had expected to hear, not what he expected at all. He stood for several minutes under Mama's constant gaze. His eyes darted from side to side. Every heart was beating. Every eye was on him,

and he knew it. Finally, the captain gave a heavy sigh, uncocked the trigger, and rammed the pistol back into the holster. He stared at Mama and then curled his lip into a smirk.

"You can thank General Sherman for this," he said.

For the first time, Mama's face showed an expression of great surprise. Captain Ross turned to go, then stopped and added, "He gave direct orders to Colonel Grierson before leaving Tennessee not to harm the Franklin family or home. You were lucky," the young officer took two steps down then looked backed again. "This time."

In only a few minutes the house was clear of Yankees. Everyone stayed frozen as if she were waiting for the curtain to fall on the last scene of a tragic play. Then Mama's knees buckled, and she crumpled to the floor. Lily and Rachel rushed to her, but Mama shooed them away with her hand. There was no time for swooning.

"Lily, go down and make sure all the soldiers are gone," she ordered.

"Quick, Rachel, open that lid," she pointed to the trunk.

With terrible dread, she obeyed her mother. Rachel was terrified of what she might see. She was afraid Papa might be dead.

Papa's body was in the grotesque position in which they had packed him, having no room to move otherwise. His head was wet with sweat, and he had passed out again. Thank goodness, Rachel thought, for Papa would have thrown back the lid to rescue Mama from the Yan-kee bullet, and all would've ended in disaster.

Just then, Lily called up.

"Dey's gone! Lizbet count sis'teen come, sis'teen gone. We safe."

"Lily, come back up," Mama called back as she jumped to her feet and began pulling on Papa. Josup appeared from somewhere, still clutching his dirty shirt, and helped Mama lift Papa out of the trunk.

"Where've you been?" Mama asked out of curiosity.

"I been standin' on de ledge," Josup grinned as the two carried Papa back to the bed.

"Oh," was all Mama said to that.

Rachel stared at the empty trunk and the pool of blood that now covered the inside.

Mama rushed back to Rachel, wrapped her arms around her, and squeezed her tightly. She kissed her hair, her forehead, her cheeks. Then she took her by the shoulders.

"Rachel, sweetheart, Papa has orders for his men that must be delivered immediately... it's of utmost importance," Mama said. "No one can do it but me. I'll take Josup and..."

"No! No, Mama!" Rachel burst into tears. "You must stay with Papa. He needs you."

"I know, dear, but there's no one else," she replied.

Rachel was quiet for a few seconds, then she took a deep breath and threw back her shoulders.

"I'll take the orders, Mama," she stated calmly.

"You, dear?" Mama looked surprised. "Oh, no, Rachel it's much too dangerous for you, sweetie."

"But, Mama," Rachel insisted. "You need to care take of Papa... and Suzanna... what if she gets worse? I can do it, Mama, I know I can."

Then Rachel thought a second and added,

"Besides, no Yankee will ever suspect that a twelve-year-old girl is on an important mission for the army."

Mama frowned, deep in thought. Maybe it was a plan that would work. But, the thought of her daughter being away from home, late at night, and in danger of running into another band of Yankees was unthinkable.

"I just can't let you do it, hon'," Mama was shaking her head.

Lily, who had been standing there listening to the whole conversation, spoke up.

"Miz Belle, she yo' chile, aw'right, but you needs to let her go. Dis here girl can do it. She too much like her mama."

"Please, Mama," Rachel began to beg. "I can do it. I really can. And I'll be fine, just fine."

This was too big a dilemma for Mama. She paced down the hall and back again, rubbing her forehead with her hand. Finally, she stopped and looked squarely at Rachel, then at Lily.

"Yes," she said. "Yes... I think it will work."

Then she surprised them both when she instructed Rachel to take off her petticoat and Lily to fetch a needle

and thread. Rachel raised her long skirt, untied the string around her waist, and let the thin, white petticoat fall to the floor. By the time she had untangled her feet from the mass of cloth, Lily was back, holding a needle with a long piece of thread.

Mama turned around and, with her back to them, retrieved the paper she had stuffed in her blouse. Then she handed it to Lily and asked her to sew the paper to the petticoat. Rachel watched with a great deal of curiosity.

Then Mama gathered Josup and Rachel around her for their instructions. The Rebel camp was near Sylamore Creek, about two miles to the southeast of the crossing.

"Near the Johnson's farm, you remember, dear, where we used to pick apples. Stay on the field road as much as possible. Keep the mules steady, Josup, and Rachel, if you do get stopped by Yankees or anybody else for that matter, tell them you're fetching a close relative, your aunt, to come see about your mother who is extremely ill." Mama spurted all this out without so much as taking a breath. "Oh, dear, this is madness."

Mama had just stared down the barrel of a Yankee gun and hadn't batted an eye. But, now she was fidgeting nervously and breathing hard. Rachel knew the best thing for all of them would be to get going.

"Mama," Rachel said softly, putting her hand on Mama's arm. "Mama, we'll be fine, just fine. We know what to do. Find Captain Wills and give him the orders, then take the road north to the Millbrook Plantation. Next morning we'll head home."

Josup finally spoke up in a voice so soft they could hardly hear him. "Missuh William, he gwine be aw'right?" Josup's eyes were moist, and Rachel knew he was very concerned about Papa. After all, he had watched Papa grow up from a tiny baby.

Mama patted Josup on the shoulder and reassured him. "Yes, Josup. I think William will be fine. Let's just pray that he will."

Josup nodded and then slipped out quietly to hitch up the mules to the wagon.

Rachel ran to her room to get her shawl. The Yankees had really made a mess, and Rachel was sure some of her things were missing. But, she would just have to get mad about it tomorrow. Right now she had too much on her mind. She was facing an unknown like nothing she had ever experienced before. She was not at all sure if she could do it. She might never make it home or see her family again. Now Rachel knew how Papa and Bud felt each time they had to return to the war. It was not glorious at all nor was it adventurous or fun. It was just downright scary. And they had both returned wounded and bleeding.

The war was no longer something far away. It had come to the Franklin front door and into their house. And now, Rachel was a part of it. In truth, she was going off to war.

14

On Angel's Wings

april, 1863

THE WAGON JERKED AGAIN, shaking Rachel out of her thoughts of the past and all the events that had brought her here. She looked back over her shoulder for the hundredth time. But there was no sound or movement as far as she could see. She strained to see in front of her down the small field road. They should've reached Sylamore Creek by now, unless they had gotten lost. Surely they weren't lost. They simply couldn't be lost. There was no time for that.

Rachel had not read the orders that she was harboring in her petticoat. But she knew it had something to do with Grierson's men and their movement south through Mississippi. Papa had mentioned cutting them off at a bridge.

Papa's men could only accomplish this if they reached the bridge first. Time was of the essence. They needed to hurry, but mules didn't understand speed.

Just ahead, Rachel could see moonlight shimmering on the ground. It was the creek. They had finally reached it. The mules hesitated when their hooves touched the water, and Josup had to coax and whistle and finally whip them across the shallow crossing.

The wagon rocked back and forth violently as they slowly moved over the rocky creek bottom. Trace-chains jangled loudly, and wagon wheels creaked. If Yankees were close, Rachel and Josup would surely be detected now. Rachel sat rigid and held on tightly so she wouldn't be pitched out of the wagon and into the cold water.

When the mules hit dry land on the opposite side, they strained against their harnesses, pushing their front legs into the soft mud, to pull the heavy wagon out of the water behind them. With a forward lurch the wagon rolled freely onto the creek bank, and they were off again. Josup guided the mules down the road that headed southeast, and they were on the last leg of their perilous journey.

The moon that had shone so brightly only a few minutes before was now hidden behind thick clouds. Josup had to trust the mules to stay on the narrow road as it was pitch-black dark, and he couldn't see a thing. The wind picked up and was rustling the trees loudly. Rachel wrapped her shawl around her shoulders. It had grown very chilly, and she knew a storm was brewing. Rachel prayed that they would reach Papa's men before the rain came.

Somewhere in the distance Rachel heard the low rumble of thunder. She was glad it sounded so far away, and she found herself relaxing her shoulders and closing her eyes drowsily. They just might beat the storm and the Yankees.

But something wasn't right. The thunder didn't stop. It only got louder. Then she realized the rumbling wasn't thunder at all, but the beating of horses' hooves.

Rachel snapped her head around and stared at Josup. He stared back with big, round eyes that were full of fear. They both feared the worst. And the rumble only got louder and closer, closer by the minute.

The heavy clouds that had blocked the moon suddenly parted and drifted away, allowing the moonlight to shine on the road once again. Rachel watched the road behind them as the pounding continued to grow louder. She wheeled around and studied the road in front. Trees hugged the sides of the narrow road closely. There was nowhere for the cumbersome wagon to go but straight ahead. Soon the horsemen, most likely Yankees, would be right on top of them.

If it were the same sixteen riders who had invaded her home, they would recognize her. The made-up story of an aunt and a sick mother would not work with them. These Yankees knew her mother was anything but sick. They would know Rachel was helping her father in some way.

Rachel envisioned being yanked from the wagon, tied up, and taken as prisoner. Maybe Captain Ross would aim his pistol at her, and she was sure she could not stare

him down like Mama. Things looked hopeless.

But suddenly, there appeared a possible escape. Rachel could see a fork in the road just ahead. To get to the Rebel camp they would need to veer right, to the south, and by the grace of God, the Yankees might possibly go left.

Josup saw it, too. He slapped the reins, and as if the mules sensed the danger, they quickly picked up their pace. The wagon wheeled past the split in the road. Surely the angels were watching over them for right past the fork was an open field, not yet planted, which gave the wagon plenty of room to get off the road. Josup pulled the reins to the left with all his might, and the wagon bumped and bounced off the road into the field. Then he pulled the mules to a stop.

Both mules and riders alike were breathing hard. They were not out of danger yet. The wagon was hidden from view by a thick row of trees from the fork in the road. But if the Yankees took the south road, as Josup had done, they would be visible as the men passed. Josup and Rachel jumped down from the wagon and hid in the trees. They listened to the ever-increasing thunder of hooves coming toward them.

Then, the horses stopped. The riders were so close Rachel and Josup could hear the men's voices, shouting and yelling at each other. What were they doing? Had the Yankees seen their wagon? Were they starting a search for them? Rachel could hardly stand the waiting. Then, just as suddenly as they had stopped, the horses took off again. But, this time the pounding began to fade, and gradually,

as Rachel held her breath, the sound of hooves could be heard no longer.

Josup and Rachel both let out a loud sigh of relief. They ran back to the wagon and climbed aboard. For the first time since leaving home Rachel spoke.

"Let's go!" was all she said.

Josup turned the mules around and got back on the road. Rachel's ears never stopped listening for the sound of those dreaded hoof-beats. They had been lucky this time. Then Rachel thought of Captain Ross's last words. "This time." Rachel's skin crawled, and she shivered under her shawl. All the Franklins had been lucky so far, but how much longer could their luck hold out? She didn't want to think about it.

"Who goes there?"

A deep voice boomed out, cutting the silence like a knife. Josup jerked back on the reins, and the mules stopped dead in their tracks. Neither Rachel nor Josup said a word. They were frozen in the darkness.

Rachel could see nothing. No movement. No signs of life anywhere. Who had said that? Where was he? Was he a Yankee or a Rebel? Her heart began to pound again, and she was afraid to breathe.

"I said, who goes there?"

The voice was even louder, and more demanding.

Again, Rachel and Josup were afraid to speak up.

"I'll shoot ya' dead right here, if ya' don't answer."

Rachel was sure that the voice did not sound Yankee, but now, it didn't matter. Whether he was friend or foe,

she had to answer.

"It's Rachel Franklin!" Rachel quickly yelled out. She certainly had not come this far to be shot for holding her tongue. "And Josup."

Then, somewhere in the darkness of the trees, a lantern was lit. It moved closer to the wagon, and Rachel could finally see a large, burly man with bristly white whiskers carrying it. He moved right up to Rachel's side and lifted the light to see her better. She sat perfectly still and allowed him to study her good. Then he raised the lantern higher and studied Josup, too.

Rachel couldn't see much, but she knew the dark object under his arm was a shotgun and that he had on a soldier's uniform. What color it was she couldn't quite tell in the darkness, although she was certain it was a lighter color than dark blue. Her heart stopped pounding with fear and started throbbing with excitement.

"Are you Confederate?" she asked shyly, taking her chances that she had found the right side.

"Hm-m-m," the man grunted. "Warn't be nothin' else. Not a yeller-bellied bluecoat, that's fer sure."

Rachel let out a deep sigh of relief, exhaustion, and downright, Praise-the-Lord happiness.

"I need to see Captain Wills," she stated her business confidently now. "It's of utmost importance."

"Well, miss, I'm sure it's awful important, for a fact," he smirked. "But I can't let ya' pass. No, ma'am, Cap'n can't be disturbed."

"But I must see Captain Wills," Rachel insisted. "I

231

have important orders for him."

The man grinned and rubbed his thick whiskers as he thought about this.

He couldn't see how a little girl and an old slave could be of any importance at all.

"Give them there orders to me, an' I'll be sure the Cap'n gets 'em," he replied and held out his hand.

"No, sir," Rachel stood firm. "I must give them to Captain Wills. Nobody else." Then she added in a voice much softer, "If you'll be so kind as to show us the way."

Now the soldier laughed out loud, making Rachel's face heat up with anger and embarrassment.

"You must show me to Captain Wills," Rachel demanded, stomping her foot on the wagon floorboard. "I have orders from Colonel Franklin, and I must deliver them now."

The laughter stopped immediately on hearing her father's name.

"Ya' say, them there orders is from Colonel Franklin?"

Rachel nodded her head, "Yes, sir."

"Well, little Reb' I'll take ya' to the Cap'n myself."

With that said, the soldier heaved himself up into the back of the wagon and directed Josup past the other picket guards. Rachel felt the tension that had kept her stiff and jumpy on this terrifying trip leave her body as she realized she was safe in Rebel hands. She wanted to say something friendly to the picket guard crouched down behind the wagon seat, but a deep whiff of him had choked back all words. She could barely catch her breath. It was easier to be downwind of the mules than close to this foul-smelling human. Rachel understood that soldiers did not get to bathe often; even so, she could not control her urge to gag. So she sat motionless and stared ahead into the darkness.

A sudden tingle of fear ran down her spine again. It was the darkness. The moon had once again vanished behind the clouds. Beyond the glow of the guard's lantern not a thing could be seen. Rachel could hardly make out the mules just in front. Something was not right. Where were the campfires? Where were the sounds of men, horses, dogs, anything? Even this late at night, there should be signs of life somewhere. Bud had once told her an army camp never slept. This one was not only asleep – it was dead. Rachel felt a whole new wave of fear cover her again like a heavy blanket.

Just then, the guard ordered Josup to pull up the mules. Rachel jerked her head toward Josup and tried to see his face, but it was too dark. She suspected he was looking straight ahead with that stone-faced look he put on when around strangers, the one that made him feel invisible. It didn't matter now, anyway. This was her mission, and Josup had done all he could to help her. Now, she was on her own.

The light from the lantern danced and flickered as the soldier heaved himself out of the wagon and jumped to the ground.

"C'mon, miss," he said as he held his free hand up to help Rachel down. The lantern was swaying in his other hand, making strange shadows on the man's face. She could see he was smiling with an almost toothless grin.

Rachel shuddered but slowly held out her hand and willed her body to move off the wagon seat. She grasped the guard's hand. It felt as rough as a dried-up corn cob but thick and strong, and she gripped it as she struggled to get her stiff, sore legs over the side of the wagon. With only the strength of his one free arm, the guard somehow managed to bring her down to the ground.

"Follow me, miss," he grunted and took off in long, brisk strides.

Rachel lifted her skirt just above her boots so she could step quickly in an effort to keep up with the huge man. She still could not see where he was taking her. Everything around them was dark and still. She was straining so hard to see the ground and watch her step that she didn't realize they were now standing in front of a large tent. It was not white like the ones she had seen pitched in the army camp but rather brown or gray or some color that blended well in the dark of night. Rachel thought everyone must be asleep for there was no light anywhere except the lantern in the guard's hand.

"Cap'n Wills, sir," the soldier called out. "Sir, there's a messenger here to see you. Says it's mighty important. Orders from Colonel Franklin."

There was some movement inside the tent. Then suddenly, the flap of the tent flew open. Rachel could see the outline of a man standing in the opening but could not see his face. Behind him was a light glowing from inside the tent.

"Come in quickly," the man ordered.

The picket guard stepped to one side and backed away. Rachel stood there staring at the guard and wondering why he wasn't going in quickly. Then she realized the order was for her.

"I said quickly!" he snapped this time.

Rachel lowered her head and slipped past the man holding the tent flap open. Once inside, she looked up to find there were two other men in the tent. One was sitting on a cot, and the other was standing over a small table, studying something that was lying there. A few seconds of shock and surprise at seeing a little girl enter passed before any of the men moved. Then, the first man closed the tent door and began fastening the buttons on his officer's coat. He was rather short and a little too plump for a man in cavalry. He seemed to be having trouble with the buttons around his middle. His hair was thinning on top but hung down below his neck in the back. He smiled nervously at Rachel who was too tense to smile at anyone.

The man on the cot, or maybe he was a boy Rachel thought, quickly sprang to his feet, reached for his coat, and fumbled to get it on. He was tall and lanky and couldn't have been more than eighteen, if that. Rachel thought he was rather handsome with blonde hair, a smooth face with only a thin, wispy mustache, and a neatly-trimmed goatee. She would have exchanged a smile with him, but he was so busy wrestling with his coat that he never looked up.

The third man, definitely much older, slowly looked up from the table and just stared at her. He was tall and thin with a heavy, black mustache and dark wavy hair

that was dirty and straggly. In the dim light of the candles on the table Rachel could not see the man's eyes, but she knew he was studying her. No one said a word.

Finally, Rachel blurted out, "I'm Rachel Franklin. I have orders from my father, Colonel William Franklin. He's wounded… so…so he sent me."

All three men seemed speechless. Again, no one spoke. Then, finally her words seemed to sink in.

"You say Colonel Franklin is wounded?" The man at the table came to life.

"How… where… what happened?" Then, as if remembering his manners, he added, "Here, miss, please have a seat." He pointed to the cot, the only thing in the tent on which to sit. The young blonde solider, having finally won the struggle with the coat, stepped aside, gestured to the cot, and smiled sheepishly at Rachel. She managed a slight smile back.

"No, thank you, sir," Rachel answered politely, eyeing the cot but preferring to stand rather than sit on it. This was no social call. It was an important mission.

"The orders, sir. I have orders from Papa…er, Colonel Franklin, and he said they were urgent. I need to give them to Captain Wills."

"I'm Captain Wills," said the man who had offered the seat. "I'll take those orders."

It was only in that split second that Rachel remembered where the orders were. She gasped out loud, then put her hand over her mouth as if to put the gasp back in. The three men looked at her, then one another, then

back at her. She stared at all three, not knowing what to do next. She couldn't lift her skirts in their presence. She couldn't tell them where the orders were. She didn't know what to do.

"Well, miss," Captain Wills broke the silence. "I'll take those orders now."

Rachel's voice trembled as she answered, "If you'll excuse me, sirs." She looked at each man in turn. "I need a moment of privacy."

"You need a… moment?" Captain Wills looked at his comrades.

Rachel thought she saw the short, plump one's mouth turn up at the corners in a suppressed smile. Her face began to heat up and turn red.

"Of privacy?" the captain finished, then shook his head. Rachel's jaw tightened as she waited. "Well, miss, if you insist."

Captain Wills nodded to his fellow officers and said, "Gentlemen, please join me outside for a. . . moment."

Whether or not they went outside and had a good laugh about her did not matter right now. As soon as the tent flap closed after the men Rachel frantically lifted up her skirt and pulled at the ties of her petticoat. The thin, white slip fell to the ground, and Rachel quickly stepped out of it. She grappled with the material until her fingers found the piece of paper. Then she carefully started to pull the threads to release the orders. Her hands were shaking, and it was almost impossible to grab the tiny thread much less break it.

237

"Lily, why do you have to sew so well?" thought Rachel to herself. Everyone knew whenever Lily mended something, it stayed mended for good. She tried biting the thread with her teeth, and just when she thought her teeth would break, the thread popped and broke. She pulled as quickly as she could to unstitch the paper until it was finally free. Holding the orders between her teeth, she stepped into her petticoat, slid it up to her waist, and clumsily tied the strings. Then she dropped her skirt, straightened it down, and took a deep breath. Out of habit, she patted her hair into place, then huffed at herself for being so silly at such a critical time.

"Captain Wills, here are the orders," called Rachel in a shaky but loud voice. "You may come back in."

The tent flap opened, and in stepped the two Rebel officers and the young solider. They did not smile or smirk but looked at the paper in her hand with dead seriousness. Captain Wills took the orders, opened the paper, and read quickly. The next minutes were a flurry of activity. The captain gave orders to each of the two men, and, in a flash, they were rounding up men to saddle horses and move out. Rachel could hear the sounds of horses neighing, hooves stomping, men shouting and running in all directions. The camp that earlier was dead was now alive with action.

Captain Wills gathered some things from the table and was about to leave the tent when he suddenly remembered Rachel. She had not moved a muscle since handing over the orders.

"We've got to move fast," he explained excitedly. "You stay here. I'll have one of my men look after you… get you what you need. You'll be safe here."

"But…" Rachel started to speak. "But, I have to get…"

"Stay here," Captain Wills demanded. "It's too dangerous for you to be on the road with Yankees about." He pointed a finger to a spot on the ground at Rachel's feet. "Stay put… that's an order."

And in the next instant, the captain was gone, leaving Rachel still trying to protest that she needed to go home. She was frozen to the spot, mouth open, but no words coming out. Maybe she stopped breathing. Maybe she was so rigid her knees locked. Maybe all the tension that was released with the orders sucked the blood right out of her head. Whatever was happening, Rachel started to feel weak. Hot and dizzy, she tried to look around the tent for the cot so she could sit down. But she didn't make it. Before she could move, the room went blurry, started to spin, and everything went black.

Rachel lay lifeless on the floor.

15
The War Comes Home

april, 1863

POP!... POP, POP!... POP! POP! POP! Rachel could hear the bullets hitting the side of the wagon. She bent down low on the seat. Josup was trying to prod the mules to go faster, but the wagon seemed to be creeping along. Pop! Pop! The bullets peppered the ground around the wheels. Rachel could see small puffs of dirt fly up with each hit. Faster, Josup, we must go faster!

She was praying and gripping the sides of the seat as tightly as she could. Afraid to look around or behind her, she kept her eyes glued to the ears of the mules. Suddenly she felt Josup push against her shoulder. She turned to see a dark red stain on the back of his shirt.

"Josup! Josup!" Rachel screamed. Josup was hit, but he continued to grip the reins and guide the mules. Wrapping her arms around his shoulders for support, she hoped he could stay on the seat. She laid her head against his arm and dared to look behind them.

There in the bed of the wagon lay Papa, wounded and writhing in pain from being jostled on the bumpy road. He was bleeding heavily from the wound in his side. Mama had wrapped her body around him, and Rachel screamed again when she saw a bloodstain on Mama's right arm, the sleeve of her pretty blue dress ripped open. Rachel dug her face in Josup's shirt. She could bear to look no longer.

Then, a sudden jolt lifted all of them off the wagon. One of the mules jerked, stumbled, and fell. Blood oozed from its side. Down went the mule, pulling the other one off course and jerking the wagon till it tipped on two wheels. It righted itself with a terrible jolt, nearly pitching them all out onto the ground. Still the bullets popped around them. Rachel screamed again and again. Blood was everywhere, everywhere! And all she could do was put her hands over her face and scream.

She woke herself up.

Rachel opened her eyes. Breathing hard, her neck and hair were wet with sweat. She was lying flat of her back looking up at a dull gray sky. But it was not the sky. It was the dirty canvas of a tent. Rachel blinked, then blinked again. She did not know where she was, but she could still hear the sound of bullets. She held her breath

and listened carefully.

Rain. It was rain pelting the tent that she heard, not bullets. Rachel let out a long breath of relief. It had been a dream, a horrible dream. She rubbed her face with her hands. It was the worst nightmare she had ever had!

But where was she?

Rachel raised up on two elbows and looked around. She was on the cot that she had declined to sit on the night before. How she had gotten there she didn't know. The last thing she remembered was standing in the middle of the tent's tiny space, alone, feeling very sick. She was fully dressed down to her muddy boots. Sitting up, she swung her legs over the side of the cot. It was all coming back to her now—the tense night journey, the smelly picket guard, the darkness, the three officers, the orders. But where was everybody? Where were Josup and the wagon?

Just then someone called out. "Miss, you aw'right in there?"

The voice startled Rachel, and she jumped.

"Oh, dear," she thought. Someone had heard her scream.

"Yes," she called back. "Yes, I'm all right, thank you very much."

"Can I gitcha' anythang, miss?" the voice called out again.

"No, no," Rachel whispered to herself. "Just go away."

Then, on second thought, she jumped up and pushed back the tent flap. There on the other side stood a small soldier, not much bigger than Rachel and certainly not

243

much older. He must have been standing outside the tent a long time because he was soaking wet with rain dripping off his big, floppy hat. He was so startled by Rachel's abrupt appearance at the door that he stumbled backwards, nearly losing his balance and falling in the mud.

"Yes, there is something you can get me," Rachel said, ignoring the boy's clumsy embarrassment. "I need to find Josup and our wagon. Can you show me where they are?"

The boy fidgeted, touched his hat but decided to keep it on his head, and tried to look at Rachel through the steady rain.

"Uh-h-h, no, miss," he managed to say. "I got orders to keep you in this here tent. But I can gitcha' some food."

"Orders?" Rachel said in disbelief. "Orders to keep me here?" She simply could not understand. She needed to go home. She needed to see about Papa and Mama and Suzanna. "I can't stay here. I must go home!"

Rachel could see that the young soldier was distraught, and although she felt sorry for him for having to stand on guard in the rain, she could not let him keep her in the tent. She would just have to find Josup and the wagon by herself, and she let him know it.

"Please, miss," the boy pleaded. "Let me fetcha' some breakfast. Then I'll see what I can do 'bout your wagon."

The rain was pouring now, and the prospect of tromping around camp in the mud looking for Josup did not look good. So Rachel let the boy win the argument. She slipped back inside the tent and waited.

Before long, breakfast arrived. Rachel did not real-

ize just how hungry she was until she opened the small, cloth bundle the soldier had brought. Supper the night before had been interrupted, and she had not had a bite since noon the day before. There were two biscuits, fairly hard but warm, a piece of fried meat of some kind, and a pot of hot, black coffee. She welcomed the warm liquid, although it was so bitter she could only take a few sips. She chewed on the biscuit but almost choked trying to swallow it down. Normally, she would have felt guilty for not eating more, but, just then, she heard horses approaching outside. Her heart raced when she heard the sound, even though her common sense told her the riders would be friend, not foe.

Rachel quickly opened the flap to see six men pulling up right in front of the tent. Her heart leaped for joy as she saw Josup following close behind them in the wagon. Josup was covered in a large piece of oilcloth to keep him somewhat dry, although now, thank goodness, the rain had slowed to a light drizzle. Rachel watched as the man on the first horse dismounted. He was dressed in a long overcoat and a big-brimmed hat that hung over his face and dripped with rain. In two big strides he was standing in front of Rachel, and when he looked up, she recognized the tall blonde solider from the night before. For some strange reason, she suddenly felt how badly she needed a bath, a hairbrush, and a fresh blouse and skirt. She wanted to duck inside the tent and hide, but she had no choice but to look him squarely in the face.

"Good mornin' Miss Rachel," he touched the brim of

his drenched hat and smiled. "I pray you had a pleasant night's sleep." His eyes had a twinkle of mockery, but his smile and voice were genuine charm.

"As good as possible, thank you very much," answered Rachel in her most polite voice.

"And a pleasant breakfast as well," he added.

"As good as possible," she repeated, not wanting to tell the truth, which would have been terribly rude.

"I do apologize, Miss Rachel," he continued, "but I haven't properly introduced myself. Corporal Andrew Carter from Louisiana." Again he touched the brim of his hat. Rachel nodded in return. And, as if they were at some social event rather than standing in the rain in front of an army tent, he continued to chit-chat. "I knew, I mean, I know your brother... from the academy. He was an upper classman. I was just a first-year cadet... still be there if it weren't for this."

Corporal Carter smiled broadly causing Rachel to return the smile. He seemed to have more to say, and although Rachel was eager to get to the wagon, she waited politely.

"I left to join up," he looked at her squarely, and Rachel realized he had very nice light-blue eyes. "They made me a corporal, comin' from the academy and all, and now I'm aide and messenger for Captain Wills."

Rachel didn't know what to say, and she didn't understand why the corporal was telling her all this. But she continued to wait patiently.

"Sorry, Miss Rachel," he stammered, touching his hat

again. "I didn't mean to bore you with all that. I came to tell you we're here to escort you home."

Rachel wanted to squeal with joy but restrained herself. Instead, she pulled her shawl up over her head and swished up her skirt to head for the wagon. But the rain had made the ground a virtual lake, and it was impossible to walk without going ankle deep in water and mud. Corporal Carter saw this and very quickly stepped to Rachel's rescue.

"If I may, Miss Rachel," he said as he whisked her off the ground and carried her the few yards to Josup and the wagon.

Corporal Carter may have looked thin and lanky, but his arms were solid and very strong. Rachel could hardly breathe as she clung to his broad shoulder. She had never been carried by a man other than Papa, and she could feel her face heat up with embarrassment. She would not look up as they passed the other men waiting on their horses, although she could feel all eyes on her. It seemed an eternity before Rachel felt herself being lifted up and onto the wagon seat.

Cpl. Carter touched his hat with a smile. "Miss," was all he said. He then turned, walked back to his horse, and mounted. The horses moved out in pairs, side by side. Josup gave the reins a snap and coaxed the mules into following the procession.

The journey home seemed much shorter than the terrifying one to the camp. It wasn't long before they had passed the heaven-sent fork in the road that had saved

their lives and the mission. Before Rachel realized it they were already crossing the creek which she thought they would never find in the dark. It had turned out to be a beautiful spring day. The rain was gone, and the sun was shining brightly. Signs of spring were everywhere. Trees were budding in pretty white, pink, and yellow hues. Wildflowers had popped out in the fields and along the road.

Rachel would have enjoyed these signs of spring if she had even noticed them. Her eyes had been glued on Cpl. Carter ever since the journey started. She watched him ride and thought how much he reminded her of Bud. The way he sat on his large horse, the squareness of his shoulders, the feel of his strong arms, and the life in his eyes were so like the big brother she adored. Rachel couldn't stop thinking about the way he had carried her, so effortlessly and smooth. Her own thoughts made herself blush and feel very fluttery in her stomach. She felt silly giving so much attention to this person she hardly knew and probably would never see again. Yet, she couldn't take her eyes off the horseman in the front.

It was only when the wagon turned onto the lane that led to her front door that Rachel's mind filled with all the worries that lay ahead. She could not bear to think of what she might find. Had Papa made it through the night? How was Mama? And what about Suzanna?

The small procession pulled up at the back of the house. No one came out to meet them. No one stood in the doorway. Rachel jumped down from the wagon as soon as it stopped and ran up the porch steps. She threw

the kitchen door open and looked around the room for Lily or Lizbet. No one was here. She didn't hear a sound in the whole house. This was strange, very strange. Where was everyone?

She raced to the stairs but stepped lightly as she scurried up them. At the top she stopped still, catching her breath and listening again. Afraid to move to her parents' bedroom, afraid of what she might learn, she closed her eyes and whispered a short prayer, gaining the courage to step forward. In the bedroom the drapes were closed, making the room very dark. Rachel's eyes could not adjust quickly, and for several minutes she couldn't see a thing. Then slowly she saw the outline of Papa's body lying in the bed. Mama was sitting on a stool beside him with her head down on the bed. Neither one of them moved as Rachel tiptoed into the room.

Her heart pounded, and her body began to shake. Her sobbing was uncontrollable. As she stood by Papa's bed, she cried as she had never cried before, until a soft, weak voice spoke up.

"Rachel, dear, it's you," Mama straightened up and pushed away from the bed. "You're back, oh dear Lord, you made it back."

Mama wrapped her arms around Rachel. They sobbed together, out of joy, out of sorrow, out of relief. Then Mama stepped back and gave Rachel her handkerchief. Rachel tried hard to stop the tears and wipe her eyes, but she thought she might never stop crying. She was afraid to look at Papa, and she was afraid to hear

249

what Mama had to say.

Mama gave Rachel a moment before she spoke.

"Papa's lost a lot of blood, dear. But we were lucky. The wound was not deep, and Lily got the bullet out," Mama sighed. Her voice was full of weariness. "He's been resting well today."

Mama turned to Papa and stroked his head. He did not move. Rachel felt the tears rise up anew. She began to sob again. Poor Papa! What pain he must have suffered! Poor Mama! What a horrible thing for her!

Mama patted Rachel and stroked her hair. "He's going to be all right, sweetheart," she said in a tone Rachel could believe. "Pray very hard. He'll be all right."

Rachel wanted to believe Mama with all her heart, but she was still sniffling and wiping her eyes when she heard someone else enter the room. It was Suzanna, standing in the doorway and holding on tightly to the door frame. She was dressed in her night clothes, looked pale as a ghost, and had a look of pure confusion on her face. Mama and Rachel were so surprised to see Suzanna out of bed that for a few minutes they both just stared at her.

"I heard horses," Suzanna said softly. Her voice was weak and hoarse. "I thought it might be Bud." She looked at Rachel and Mama, then past them at the bed. "Is that Bud? Is he here?" Her eyes searched their faces. "What's going on?"

Finally realizing it was Suzanna and that she shouldn't be out of bed, Mama rushed to her and wrapped her arms around Suzanna's shoulders. She led Suzanna to a chair

by the window and opened the drapes just enough to let in a little light.

"What's happened? Tell me, what's happened?" she kept saying over and over.

Mama turned to Rachel. "Please, dear, go down and ask Lily to fix a tray of something for you and Suzanna. You must be starved, and I know Suzanna needs to eat."

In truth, Rachel was starved, and she welcomed the chance to leave while Mama related the long, terrible story to Suzanna. Rachel raced back down the stairs and into the kitchen. But where was Lily? Where was Lizbet? Where were the other girls? There was no sign of them anywhere in the house.

Rachel stepped out on the back porch. Josup had disappeared with the mules and wagon into the barn. The six horsemen were unsaddling their horses in the shade of the oaks in the side yard. They would need feeding as well. Surely Lily was in the cookhouse already baking up some biscuits or roasting a hen. She ran across the yard, expecting the wonderful aromas of Lily's cooking to reach her any moment, but, to her great disappointment and annoyance, no Lily, no Lizbet, nothing cooking in the cookhouse. Rachel was now extremely hungry and very irritated with this search. She planned to do a fair share of fussing whenever she did find them. Off she stomped to the smokehouse.

That's when she spotted Lily walking toward the house from the slave quarters. Rachel thought that was strange since Lily and Lizbet lived in the main house and

never went to the slave cabins. Rachel called out to Lily, but she did not stop or look up. She headed directly to the house and went inside. Rachel rushed after her, in no mood to play chase. She opened the backdoor and was just about to let fly a whole mouthful of fussing, when she saw Lily's face. Rachel stopped dead in her tracks, her mouth dropped open, and not a word would come out. She quickly forgot about her growling stomach.

Lily was sitting at the table facing Rachel. She stared at Rachel but did not appear to see her. Lily's eyes were stone cold and black, and strangest of all, they brimmed with tears. Her jaws were clenched tightly, and her chin was quivering. Never in her life had Rachel seen Lily cry. Lily fussed a lot and ranted at times, but this was a Lily she had never seen, and it scared her.

"Lily, what's wrong? Rachel managed to speak. "What's wrong?"

Lily's head moved slightly from side to side as if she were looking for the person whose voice she heard. Then she looked directly at Rachel.

"My baby's gone," she said through clenched teeth. "Gone, ya' hear. My chile, she gone." And then she broke into the most horrible wail one could ever hear. It was the cry of grief that only mothers cry when something has happened to their baby. She put her hands to her head, rocked back and forth, and wailed.

Rachel felt her heart flip-flop in her chest. What was happening? What was she talking about? Where was Lizbet?

"Lily, please, gone where?" she begged, now frantic

to learn about her friend. She put her hands on Lily's arms and shook her. "Where's Lizbet? What's happened? Please, Lily, tell me."

Through the wailing and the gasping Lily spurted out, "She gone. She run away. She gone to de Yankees. She gone to freedom."

Stunned, Rachel let go of Lily and stood staring at the crazed woman in disbelief. She couldn't believe that Lizbet had run off. She loved Lizbet, and she thought Lizbet loved her. They were best friends, and this was their home. How could Lizbet ever leave here? Where would she go?

Suddenly Rachel remembered a day that Lizbet and she had sat on the back porch. Lizbet had talked about being free, and her words came back to Rachel now as clearly as if it were yesterday. "I don't knows what I do. But I be free to do it."

Rachel knew then that it was true. Lizbet had gone to freedom. But what would she do? Lizbet could not take care of herself. And what would the Yankees do to her? Rachel knew she and Lily must do something. They must get her back. But how?

"Mama," thought Rachel. "Mama will know what to do."

And as if Mama had read her thoughts, she appeared in the doorway.

"What's all this commotion in here?" Mama looked puzzled at the two weeping faces before her. "What's happened? Rachel... Lily... what's the matter?"

Lily tried to speak, though her chest was heaving in great spasms. She blurted out, "My baby... gone. My Lizbet... my chile... she gone fo'evuh."

Mama knelt by Lily's side and wrapped her arms around her to calm her. Lily did calm down somewhat, changing from wails to quiet sobs. Rachel stood nearby sobbing, too, but still convinced they needed to take action.

"Mama," she pleaded. "We must go after her. Please, Mama, we have to get Lizbet back."

Mama stood up and straightened her stiff back. Her arms were tired from comforting, her hands were tired from wiping away tears and blood, her body was tired, just plain tired. There were so many who needed her right now.

"There's nothing we can do, sweetheart," Mama sighed. "Lizbet has chosen to run away. We'll pray she'll be all right."

Then Mama turned to Lily. "I'm so sorry, Lily. So sorry. I wish I could do something."

"Yes'm," Lily answered. She wiped her face with her apron. She took a deep breath and stood up. "I need fix this here chile sum'pun to eat." And as if none of this had ever happened, Lily went to work as usual, grabbing pots and pans and knives.

Rachel sank into a chair, putting her head on the table. She knew Mama was right. Lizbet had chosen to run away. She had wanted freedom, and there was nothing any of them could do to get her back. Rachel would pray for Lizbet every day. That was all she could do about any of the horrible things that were happening to them.

Rachel hoped that one day she would see her friend again, but she knew in her heart she never would. The days with Lizbet were gone as were the days of carefree, happy times—never to return.

As a pendulum swings up high to the top of one side, drops down, and swings up high to the opposite side, so did the events in the life of the Franklin family begin to change. They had ridden the rise of one bad thing after another until they could hardly stand any more. Now events seemed to be swinging on the side of hope and good news. Two weeks passed quickly, and in that time Suzanna got well. Once again her face had a healthy glow, and she was able to help Mama take care of Papa. Her laughter alone made Rachel feel better.

Papa was recovering as well. With Mama's loving care, Lily's concoctions, and the attention of Rachel and Suzanna, he soon went from walking around the bedroom to taking walks in the yard. He already spoke of things he needed to do around the plantation, getting the fields ready for planting, making repairs to this or that. He never spoke of returning to the war, although Rachel suspected he was only sparing all of them from the worry that kind of talk brought.

Rachel's mission had been a success, at least in part. Papa received a report from Captain Wills stating that the bridge had been secured by his men in time to stop

the Yankees from crossing and destroying the train depot. They had not, however, been able to capture Grierson and his men, and the elusive Yankees were still on the loose, moving deeper into Mississippi. Along with the report was a separate envelope addressed to Rachel. To her surprise, it was a letter from Cpl. Carter, making her blush as she read it. He called her a courageous little Rebel, praised her brave effort, and, in closing, asked her to write to him. Would she dare to write him? She had figured out that he must be only four, maybe five, years older than herself. But, this was not a decision she could make on her own. She would have to talk to the wiser, older, more experienced Suzanna.

Rachel still worried about Lily. The housegirls, Jo and Mott, and most all the other field workers had slipped away with Lizbet, but Lily never mentioned any of them again. She went about her work silently. Unlike before, Lily didn't fuss or complain, even though her work load had increased. Rachel wondered why Lily had not gone with Lizbet, and one quiet afternoon while the two of them were in the kitchen, she had to ask.

"Dis my home," Lily answered in a firm voice. "Dis where I bo'n. Dis where I die. I don't know nuthin' else. I got nowheres else to go."

It was hard for Rachel to understand the complicated way her family's lives were so intertwined with the lives of Lily and Josup, yet so separated. She might never understand if she lived to be a hundred, but she was thankful that Lily and Josup had chosen to stay. She was glad this was their home.

Then, on a quiet afternoon in the first days of May, the best thing of all happened. Papa and Rachel were sitting on the porch enjoying the warm spring breeze when they heard a rider coming toward the house. Rachel's sense of dread was stirred up as she listened to the hooves get closer and closer.

"Oh, Lord, please don't let it be a messenger," Rachel thought to herself. "Please don't be bad news." Riders usually meant bad news, bad news about Bud or reasons for Papa to go away. She wanted neither.

Papa tensed in his chair, his hand closed around the bandage on his side, as he listened intently. The rider was slowing but coming around to the back of the house. Rachel and Papa both froze as the horse came into view.

It was Bud. Oh, blessed day! It was Bud. He steered the horse toward the porch, pulled to a dusty halt, and jumped off. Rachel practically leaped at him in her excitement. Papa stood but waited for Bud to come to him. After Bud dropped his armful of little sister back onto the porch, Rachel went running to tell Mama and Suzanna. What excitement and joy filled the Franklin house!

It was the first time in many, many months that the whole Franklin family sat at the dining table together. They all couldn't take their eyes off Bud. He looked older, almost weathered. His hair was long and wild. His beard had thickened and needed a good trim. His uniform was

tattered and dirty, but he looked wonderful to the people who loved him so. Everyone listened intently as he relayed tales of his movements and encounters with the enemy. Bud was always careful not to give too many details so as not to upset the ladies. He would be more specific in private with Papa.

Bud had only a few days to be at home. He was on his way to Vicksburg to help defend the city against Grant's advances there. He had heard news of Papa and wanted to see for himself if everything was all right. Rachel knew that they would have to face another painful departure, but it was worth all the tears to spend a few days, even a few hours, with Bud.

Three wonderful, fun-filled days passed quickly, and the terribly sad morning came for Bud to leave. Everyone was up early, helping Bud pack as much on his horse as the poor animal could stand. There was much nervous chatter as no one wanted to think about goodbye. But the time finally came for Bud to mount up. The Franklins had lived through this scene too many times before. Rachel wondered how many more times Bud would have to leave, how many more tears would be shed, how long this horrible war was going to last. She felt as if her whole life would be one tearful goodbye after another.

As predictable as the rising of the morning sun, Papa was also gone again before summer was over.

16

After the Storm

october, 1865

RACHEL SMILED AS SHE FOLDED THE LETTER she had just finished reading and slipped it back into the envelope. The breeze blowing through the open window of the parlor was still warm but smelled of autumn. She closed her eyes and breathed in a deep, deep breath. Suddenly the breath was knocked out of her as a small body rammed into her stomach. She gasped, opened her eyes, and saw the small head of wavy black hair in her lap. She mussed the soft locks with her hands and laughed. The small face looked up at her and laughed too.

"Ra-chee, come p'ay," he begged in his little child's voice. "Come p'ay, p'ease!"

Rachel looked into his twinkling eyes, beautifully green like his Grandmother Belle's. He amazed Rachel, so full of life, so full of energy. He kept the whole household on their toes.

"So, there you are, you little rascal," Mama said as she entered the parlor, "running away from me again." She grabbed the squealing child around the middle and jiggled him, making him scream with laughter. "You know it's time for your nap."

"No, MamaBelle, no!" he shrieked. "No nap!" And he clung to Rachel's skirts while Mama pulled him away.

Rachel was being tugged and pulled fiercely by the clinging child, but everyone was laughing. Then Rachel took the small face in her hands and spoke to him gently.

"Now, lil' Jay," she said, "you be a good boy for MamaBelle, and after your nap, I promise to play hide-and-go-seek."

His eyes lit up. He quickly let go of Rachel and let Mama whisk him up into her arms. Lily was soon by Mama's side to help carry the bundle of energy up to his bed. Like all the Franklin women, Lily doted on the precious child.

"Yes, Rachee, yes," he squealed as he was taken out of the room. "I be good boy. I be good boy."

Rachel watched as Mama and Lily left with their wiggly bundle. They all loved that little boy so much. Since the day he was born, February 24, 1864, he had brought complete joy to the family. Suzanna had chosen the name Jefferson (after her father) William (after Papa) Franklin. With such

a mouthful of a name, it wasn't long before he became just Jay. What a blessing this beautiful little boy was! Rachel knew he was a reminder to them all that life goes on, and he was just the breath of life that they all needed.

It was six months before Bud had been able to see his son. On a much-needed leave, Bud had been allowed to come home for a few days that August. Rachel had never seen Bud so proud and excited about anything in his life as when he held his little baby. For the first time Bud talked of giving up the war and staying with his family, so many soldiers were doing that. The desertion rate was running high. Rachel couldn't understand why he didn't just do it, stay with them. His family needed him. Hadn't he done enough? Surely, he had done his fair share. She wanted to plead with him to quit the war, but she knew it would do no good. Even though Bud wanted nothing more than to be with his family, she also knew he would never quit.

Parting was always sad, but this time when Bud had to leave, it was different. Bud was different. He took an extra long time with each of them to say his goodbye. He lingered with each hug longer than usual. He whispered loving words to each of them. He was sad, so sad, as if his heart were truly breaking. When he rode away that morning in August, it was the last time any of them would ever see him.

Bud died on November 30, 1864, at the Battle of Franklin, Tennessee. The battle had been a last desperate effort by the Army of Tennessee to recapture Nashville, and thus the state, hoping to turn the tide of the lost Confed-

erate Cause. It was a horrible defeat for the Southerners with an unbelievable casualty rate. It was called a bloodbath by some who were there.

Papa brought his son home and buried him in the family cemetery under the oaks beside the graves of his paternal grandparents. Less than ten yards away from those graves was a fresher one, the grave of dear old Josup. In times of so many unnatural, untimely deaths, it was strange and sad that here was one who had died a natural death of old age. Josup had been a constant part of the Franklin family for as long as any of them could remember. Papa insisted that Josup be laid to rest under the oaks near the Franklin family.

Papa could not speak of what had happened on that fateful day in Franklin. He had been on the battlefield with Bud, but by some miracle, Papa had been spared, escaping with a leg wound that would cause him to limp the rest of his days. He could not tell Mama or Suzanna what Bud's last hours had been like. Maybe one day he would share some of the story, in his own time, in his own way.

Mama, of course, was stricken with grief. She could barely withstand losing her only son. Rachel feared her mother might close the drapes and hide away in her bedroom as so many mothers had done. But, instead, she threw her whole being into her small grandson. She turned her grief into love for him, doting on him and, perhaps, reliving the days when she had raised a little boy.

There were no words that could comfort Suzanna. She was like an empty shell. There was no life in her eyes,

no joy in her heart. The only thing that kept her going was her little son. She loved him too much to give up on life. Every day she went to Bud's grave and sat there for hours, sometimes laying her body over the neatly piled dirt. Rachel worried about Suzanna, but Mama had reassured her that time and love would eventually heal Suzanna's broken heart.

Rachel had been outraged to learn the events that led to Bud's death. To her, it seemed a senseless attack against a Union force that was strong and entrenched. It was a suicide attempt that basically wiped out the Army of Tennessee. So many brave men were sacrificed, and for what? By the time of this battle, the balance of the war had already tipped in favor of the Union, and the Confederacy didn't have the strength to level it, much less triumph.

By November 1864, the Union had control of the Mississippi River from its source to the Gulf. Grant's Army of the Potomac had danced its way around General Lee's Army of Northern Virginia to within just miles from Richmond. Atlanta had fallen to Sherman, and his army was marching to the sea right through the heart of the South. The Confederacy was crumbling; yet, General Hood, commander of Bud's Army of Tennessee, had plunged his men into an attack that seemed doomed from the start.

Rachel wanted to scream that Bud had died in vain, but she knew to say as much would dishonor him. He would not have believed it was all in vain. He believed he was fighting for his family, for his land. He had believed in The Cause with all his heart. Giving it all his strength

and bravery, he had paid for it with his life.

And life went on. Bud lived on in his young son. Not only did Little Jay have his father's looks, his handsome features and dark wavy hair, but he already showed signs of Bud's reckless behavior and zest for life. Rachel would devote herself to helping Suzanna teach Little Jay about his father and keeping the memory of Bud alive forever.

Rachel sighed and fought back tears. She couldn't think about Bud without having to wipe her eyes. Taking a deep breath, she remembered the letter she still held in her hand. This made her smile. She opened a small wooden box and tucked the letter inside with the other letters from Andrew Carter. She had been corresponding with the young solider since he had asked her to write to him. Although Rachel had not seen him in almost two years, she remembered everything about him, his face, the way he rode his horse, and especially the way his arms felt when he had carried her over the mud. After the war Andrew had returned to his home in Louisiana to help his family get the farm running again. He had not had an opportunity to return to Mississippi and, perhaps, visit with the Franklins, but he would as soon as it was possible. The prospect of a visit from Andrew was both exciting and terrifying to her. What would they say to each other? What would Mama and Papa think?

Before the war, this letter writing would have been inappropriate for a girl not quite fifteen. But this was a new world. The rules, those silly rules that had once ruled Rachel's life, were not important in a world that was devastated, torn, grieving, and struggling to rebuild itself. Life was no longer about manners, white gloves, or tiny appetites. This was no longer her mother's world, and it never would be again.

The storm of war had hit, and it had left more destruction and death than the nation could ever have imagined. Families, like the Franklins, who had weathered the storm and survived, were a strong people, a people who could build a stronger nation, a better nation. There was hope, and hope was the heart of life.

The End

About the Author

For twenty-seven years Nancy has been teaching children to read. During this time she has read thousands of children's stories with her students and her granddaughters. Combining this love for reading and her love for writing she decided to write her own stories that she hoped children would enjoy.

Nancy lives in Memphis, Tennessee, with her husband, Earl. Their two daughters and four granddaughters also live in the city. She has a Bachelor's degree from Arkansas State University and a Master's degree in education from the University of Memphis. She currently teaches at Presbyterian Day School. She loves playing the piano, and on Sunday mornings can be found playing at her church.

Nancy is an avid reader of the Civil War, and she wanted to share the events of this war with young readers. The desire to create a story that older children and teens would not only enjoy, but could use to understand this American war was a rewarding challenge that resulted in her first book, *Rebel in Petticoats*.

Printed in the United States
124935LV00004BA/2/P

9 780980 028560